THE MASTER OF CHAOS

and Other Fables

THE
MASTER
OF
CHAOS

and Other Fables

PAULINE MELVILLE

SANDSTONE PRESS

First published in Great Britain in 2021 by
Sandstone Press Ltd
PO Box 41
Muir of Ord
IV6 7YX
Scotland

www.sandstonepress.com

Singing in the Dark Times was first published by Unbound,
2018; *Anna Karenina and Emma Bovary Discuss their Suicides*
was first published by Electric Literature, 2021.

ISBN: 978-1-913207-54-0
ISBNe: 978-1-913207-55-7

Sandstone Press is committed to a sustainable future.
This book is made from Forest Stewardship Council ® certified paper.

Cover design by Jason Anscomb
Typeset by Biblichor Ltd, Edinburgh
Printed and bound in Great Britain by Clays Ltd, Elcograf S.p.A

For Angus

And for the Melville tribe in and out of Guyana

CONTENTS

THE MASTER OF CHAOS

We arrived late at night in Georgetown, capital city of Guyana, and stood outside my grandmother's enormous white wooden house with its latticed verandas and galleries. My father rang the bell.

'Mohammed. Lock up de dogs,' a voice commanded from an upper window.

We waited until the night watchman had rounded up the dogs which were slavering behind the fence. My grandmother came down to unlock the gate. She walked towards us, a handsome, mahogany-skinned woman, slender and well-proportioned with a baggy dramatic face and permanent dark circles under her eyes. She wore a simple blouse and elegant calf-length cotton pants. The glowing tip of her cigarette traced red hieroglyphics in the black night air as she beckoned us in:

'Come in quickly. I hear thunder.'

My mother and father went in first. I followed them. I had not met my grandmother before. At fifteen I was proud of the first few wispy hairs of my moustache. I stepped forward to shake her hand but she had already turned and dashed back inside to cover the TV with a pillow-slip in case lightning struck. We waited in the entrance lobby with our bags while she disappeared upstairs, going from room to room around the house covering various electrical appliances with cloths and hanging towels over the mirrors.

'If lightning strikes a mirror – you dead,' she announced as she came down and ushered us into the spacious front room where she moved from window to window, cigarette between her lips, closing the jalousies.

'So you're Guilford are you? My only grandson.' She scrutinised me for a moment or two with an air of disappointment before turning to my parents. 'I hate thunder. I can't stand it.' As she spoke the lights dipped and the house sank into darkness. 'Look at that. The voltage. Low voltage. The lights are going. I hate this country. This country is a mess. Mess? It's a toilet bowl. Oh God, why did you have to give us this government?'

There was a magnificent humour in her theatrical depression as she threw herself back onto the sofa and crossed her legs. The lights gained strength again.

My father addressed her with affection. 'Well, you'all voted them in, Mother.'

'I have never met anyone in this country who is sane,' she proclaimed with a mixture of pride and scorn, dismissing my father's comment with a gesture. She drew on her cigarette. 'They are all crazy. Someone should take all de politicians and put them on an island in the Corentyne. No water. No electricity. No food. Let them survive. "Prosperity is round de corner", they say. It always round de blasted corner.' She paused and then: 'How did he die?'

We had brought my grandfather's body back from England for him to be buried in his homeland. According to legend, men of African descent fly back to Africa after their death. Typically, he had flown in the wrong direction.

'A heart attack,' said my father.

She looked momentarily saddened. Then she moved towards the window, pulled the jalousie slats apart and threw the cigarette stub into the garden.

'Pansy my cook doesn't like me to smoke in de house.'

My grandfather was a gambler. He came from that generation of men in the old British Guiana who were graceful simulacra of the British gentleman, a charming, mocking shadow of the real thing. In that part of the world the past sometimes succeeds in pushing the present out of the way. My grandfather was tall, slim with a pale brown complexion the colour of agate. He liked to wear dark glasses even when it was raining and kept a black silk opera hat that folded down into his suitcase. He smoked cigars and of all the rum in the world he preferred El Dorado along with his favourite snack of grilled peanuts.

He used to visit us in England but never stayed long. Sometimes when he took off his sunglasses I would catch his eye and the twinkle in it confirmed an affinity between us. People observed that, as I grew taller, I looked more and more like him. Occasionally, he took me with him when he gambled. I remember a damp room in Tottenham where I looked on as his long-fingered brown hand unfurled like the wing of an archangel to cast the dice on the cheap veneer coffee table.

His dice were unusual. They were the Crown and Anchor dice, popular with eighteenth-century seamen. Instead of being marked with one to six pips they had the card suits, spade, club, heart and diamond carved on four sides and then a red crown and a black anchor on the other two. Players use a special board marked with pictures of each suit and the crown and anchor. My grandfather's dice were light, knuckle-bone

3

weight and yellow ivory in colour. He told me they were made from the bones of a gambling friend, an Amerindian man who had died in the swampy interior of the Mazaruni River. He thought they brought him luck. As did a constellation to the upper left of Orion when it rose in the night sky. He pointed it out to me one night. The constellation of twins Castor and Pollux represented his birth sign, Gemini, but he told me that the Aztecs knew it as the constellation of the Frog. The two bright stars that represented the twins' heads in Western mythology became the two eyes of the Frog for the Aztecs. He preferred the Aztec version.

'Are you superstitious, Grandpa?' I asked.

'Only on Tuesdays,' he replied.

Another time, when he was having a run of luck, he smuggled me into the Chandos Club in Mayfair. As a twelve-year-old boy I was not allowed into the main area of the casino so I stayed in the cloakroom nestling amongst alpaca overcoats that smelled faintly of tobacco and expensive aftershave. From there I could see everything. At the gaming table my grandfather had a monkish austerity. He was an ascetic of the casino. The subdued glow of soft lighting caught his high cheekbones. His dark glasses hung on a thin gold chain around his neck. His eyes were bright and watchful. Each win was a glimpse of heaven through the laws of mathematics, as if the roof of some giant astronomical observatory had rolled back to reveal the vastness of a star-studded night sky and the eternal order of the universe. He had a dislike of the everyday world outside. It boiled with emotions and daylight and distress. Once inside he gave himself over to the calm atmosphere of the casino with its satanically polite croupiers, those servants of the infinite reach of fate.

He talked to me once about chance and fate as we waited in the rain for a bus to Lewisham.

'Chance is random. Fate is not. Fate has a plan and fate wins in the end,' he said while the rain drummed on his umbrella. 'But chance allows you to think you can escape fate for a little while. Look. Here come de bus. We in luck.'

And that was what he enjoyed. Bucking fate.

For a light-skinned 'red' man in British Guiana, barriers presented themselves. He worked first as a clerk for Sandbach Parker and then for Booker. Despite his remarkable accounting skills and his gift for mathematics, the top posts eluded him. They were available only to white Englishmen. There seemed to be no way of escaping this particular fate and he felt eviscerated, unmanned by it – until, that is, he discovered gambling.

Gambling, contrary to public perception, was for my grandfather a way of controlling his own destiny. The decisions were his and his alone. Gambling does not care about the past. No game depends or builds on the previous one. Losing is bad but there is always another opportunity, that fresh start, the optimist's clean sheet, the new dawn and undiscovered Eden. When he lost everything and only had one twenty dollar bill left, he did not see his decision to stake that last sum as an act of desperation or foolhardiness. He saw it as a test of courage. It was the act of a brave man. Did he have the nerve to risk everything? Yes, he did. He was the captain going down with the ship. He was the commander sacrificing his own life for those of his troops. And the inevitable financial loss? Well, it was an acceptable martyrdom. It was worth it to become a man again.

Newly married, he grasped his young wife's hands as they stood under the jacaranda tree outside the white latticed fence of their house and he swore that she would eventually be prosperous beyond her wildest dreams.

'Oh yes, indeed,' sighed my grandmother, rolling her eyes. But she adored him and fished in her purse once again to push a few thousand dollars into his hand.

In the end, with a confetti shower of promises, he left his wife and two children – my father and my aunt Selma – to travel the world as a professional gambler. He was gone for years at a time. At irregular intervals he would turn up or sometimes various amounts of money would appear in Grandmother's bank account. Fortunately, the house had belonged to her family. She kept tight hold of the deeds and she was shrewd enough not to let him gamble them away. But the household gradually went into decline. Furniture was sold. School fees went unpaid. Fewer staff were employed.

Meanwhile, Grandfather's success at cards – and he had some successes – was a way of putting order on chaos and becoming, briefly, Master of Chaos, as he termed it. But the mastery only lasted for a while. Chaos and disorder disrupted his life outside the casino. Rents were forfeited. Mistresses were abandoned. For a while his consort was a red-haired French woman, obscene and erotic, who wore purple and had a dread of fire. She deserted him because he left his cigar stubs burning in the house. In Port O'Spain he lived on his wits, eating sardines from a tin in a room that consisted entirely of bare boards. When things were going well, he took up residence on the third floor of Claridge's Hotel in London and started every evening with a chilled Italian white wine. In Lagos he was forced to live on the street. But that did not trouble him. He travelled further and gambled more. He brushed all domestic stuff aside and devoted himself to the

6

requirements of order, the sublime pattern of infinity and fate itself.

At the end of his life I accompanied Grandfather to the seedy Oasis and Stars gambling den in Peckham. He was already dancing on the edge of extinction. That night he lost heavily and left the table. He was exhausted. Tiny red capillaries showed up in the yellowish whites of his eyes. But even as he lost on the last throw, he stood up smiling. For on defeat the slate is wiped clean. He went to the bar and ordered his favourite El Dorado rum. Within seconds, as the liquor hit the back of his gullet it was all to play for again. Cleansed and absolved, he could start afresh. The whole world was ahead of him.

People at the bar had not noticed, until he keeled over, that he wore no shoes.

Waking on that first morning in Georgetown I found myself in a bedroom full of light and air in a city built of space. The house was like a box kite anchored to the ground. Demerara shutters opened to welcome the soft trade winds. Gauzy curtains tossed in the window. Mosquito netting ballooned like a ship's sails in the breeze. Later in the morning the same nets were transformed by a maid who twisted them into white tornados and left them hanging over the frame. Unlike London, weighed down with stone and concrete, the houses in this city seemed poised to fly upwards as if the whole city could take flight and alight elsewhere. To me, everything felt ethereal and insubstantial. A phantom city.

I left my bed to look out of the window. A paved backyard was lined with anthurium and dragon-tongue shrubs. Two giant Victoria Regina lily pads, like green flan cases, floated on the surface of a stagnant pond. And then an unexpected sight made me catch my breath. On the inside window sill just in front of me sat a tiny exquisite frog, pale gold in colour and not more than an inch long. Black eyes, disproportionately large, protruded from either side of its head. I could just detect a pulse in its throat. I held my breath as I watched. Quite without warning it gave a staggering leap, its back legs stretching out behind it and landed on grandfather's Crown and Anchor board which I'd left on the bedside table. It squatted there delicate and motionless on the red 'hearts' sign. Not wanting to disturb it I crept away into the bathroom to dress. When I came out it had gone.

Downstairs in the kitchen my grandmother stood by the open window with a telephone to each ear. She was talking to the bank on one phone and ordering a coffin on the other:

'I will need two hundred thousand dollars in cash. What do you mean I don't have it?' She rolled her eyes and turned to me as I came down the stairs: 'What is wrong with these banking people?' She put her hand over one phone and spoke down the other: 'Not de most expensive coffin and not too cheap. I will come and inspect it this afternoon.'

My father appeared.

'Mother, we can use the coffin he was shipped down in. It's very grand. You don't need to buy another.'

Outside the sky began to boil with grey clouds and there was a tropical downpour. A maid went running out to snatch washing off the line at the back. Grandmother finished her argument with the bank, slammed down the phone and glared through the window at the inclement weather. Then she turned to Pansy the cook who was scouring pans at the sink.

'Don't serve us any of that hard-arsed meat at the funeral tea, Pansy.'

8

Pansy the cook was squat and surly. Her plaited hair had the texture of a scouring pad and she wore something akin to a nurse's uniform with a striped pinafore.

'And not too much chow mein.' Grandmother talked as she busied herself putting some crockery back in the cupboard. 'I don't like the Chinese. As soon as Chinese came to this neighbourhood all the stray dogs disappeared off de road. And the rats too. Four were found in a jar in the Chinese restaurant. I'll wait till the rain stops and then I'm going to take a taxi and see Father Gordon. Would you bring us coffee in the front room just now, Pansy?'

In the front room my mother was peering through the open jalousies at the torrential rain. The sound of an ambulance siren swept past on the road outside.

A worried expression passed over my mother's face. 'Sounds like an accident or something.'

'Not at all. Nothing of the sort.' Grandmother sat down on the sofa and fanned herself with the newspaper. 'That is an ambulance that drives up and down the road all day. There is nobody in it. The man just likes transporting himself up and down de road sounding his siren. Go and fetch my glasses, Guilford dear. They are upstairs by my bed. I want to read the paper.'

I made my way through a maze of galleries and passageways upstairs until I found the bedroom with the glasses. From another part of the house where she had separate quarters I could hear the trilling laugh of my Aunt Selma who was on the telephone. I had met her the night before. She was fifty-six years old, hugely fat with pouchy cheeks, and wore her crinkly hair in two grey plaits that came down in front of her ears. She had come stomping towards me with open arms crooning as she spoke:

'Oh this is my little nephew. Hello my darling, my little sweetie-pie. Come and sit by me.' She patted the seat next to her and to my annoyance cooed over me as if I were a small child. However, within minutes she exhibited a fit of bad temper and stood up and shouted through the open window at the night watchman because the dogs were barking. The outburst was followed by an apologetic titter. My mother told me that Aunt Selma had never married, fearing that any children might inherit the rogue gambling gene which had destroyed their family life. She occupied herself with organizing cultural activities and charity events.

I came back downstairs with the glasses. My grandmother had an irritated expression on her face as she listened to Selma's laughter.

'That girl never stops talking. She always on de phone,' complained Grandmother. Then she yelled:

'Selma. Come down and play snakes and ladders with your nephew. He's bored.'

'Mother.' Selma screamed from upstairs and her foot could be heard stamping on the floor above. 'Can't you hear that I am on de phone. I am talking.'

Grandmother ignored the tantrum and turned her irritation on me:

'These glasses you gave me don't work. They are trick ones.'

Then she put down the paper with a sigh and sipped her coffee.

'Our life used to be so different. Oh, how I miss those early days. Everything was elegant. Your grandfather sat at the head of the table. Your great-aunt Albertha made all the lace for the edging on the tablecloths. To clean the table we had a tiny silver dustpan and a brush with a silver top to sweep away the crumbs. But your grandfather, bless him, was a renegade and disappeared.' She sighed. 'Then everything went to pot. My family helped but the money's finished now and everything's gone to the dogs. We livin' like . . . ghosts.' Her voice trailed off.

Earlier that morning there had been an almighty row between Grandmother and Selma when she informed Selma that the funeral was very expensive and that, therefore, they would have to get rid of either Pansy the cook or Mohammed, the night watchman. They could no longer afford both. In fact, really it should be both of them that went. There was no more money in the bank. Selma exploded with rage:

'So you mean, Mother,' she bellowed, 'that we have to choose between starving to death without a cook or being murdered in our beds without a night watchman?'

For the first time I saw my grandmother diminished and defeated as she tried to placate her daughter.

When she had finished reading the paper Grandmother left with my father to visit the priest. A few minutes later Selma appeared downstairs looking distracted, a snakes and ladders board under her arm. She had unearthed some board games from somewhere and expected me to play a variety of childish games. After a warning frown from my mother, I submitted. There was a gleam in Selma's eye as we played. She leaned forward, her foot joggling to and fro with anxiety, biting her fingernails, her grey plaits brushing the coffee table. When she won she shrieked with triumph and brandished the dice in the air.

On the day of the funeral yet another violent tropical storm burst over town. It was rainy season and there were frequent downpours. We gathered, all dressed in black, on the wooden verandah that surrounded the ground floor of the house. Selma, wearing elbow-length black gloves and exuding a musky perfume, carried a large black umbrella with a heavy fringe. She clucked and tut-tutted with impatience as she waited for the hearse. At ten past ten it arrived.

'Don't brush against the yellow allamanda,' said Grandmother as we made our way down the drive. 'There's a nest of marabunta hornets in it. If they start buzzing about everyone must stay still until they settle or you will be stung. I ain' carryin' anyone to no hospital.'

The rain stopped as suddenly as it had started. A melancholy white mist shrouded Le Repentir burial ground. We walked down the avenue of giant royal palms. The tall trees were stricken with some disease that had turned the drooping foliage mangy and yellow. The cemetery was flooded after the storm. The marble mausoleums looked as if they were floating, allowing the dead to move about below and change places. Grandfather was lowered into his grave with a splash. Grandmother stared down at the coffin for a few minutes, tears in her eyes. She was holding Grandfather's favourite Crown and Anchor dice in her hand. She had wanted to throw them into the grave so that he could play for eternity but, under the eye of the priest, she lost her nerve and gave them to me:

'Look after these for me, dear.'

When the funeral was over she instructed the undertaker to check the next day to make sure grave-robbers had not taken the body out and stolen the ornate coffin. Finally, she led the funeral party away to the waiting cars.

*

The funeral tea was held in the living room with its gleaming polished floor of greenheart wood. Grandmother held court with her usual grace. The Rodriguez boys, invited for my benefit as we were much the same age, stood there with their wide smiles. Their mother delicately removed a strand of cucumber from her teeth as she explained why, to everyone's astonishment, she had returned to Guyana from a prosperous life in America.

'Yes. I came back from America. You ask why? Well, just observe the American middle-class children. Everything lookin' fine and dandy. They polite. They all ready and dressed in time for school. They have a glass of milk and a cookie. They attend endless activities – summer camp, swimming club, school proms. They are neat and well-behaved. Then when they're sixteen they come home and shoot their parents. Well I have two sons getting to that age. I can't take de risk.'

Caso, a sly, wizened old walnut of a man, a gambling buddy of Grandfather's, grabbed my arm to whisper in my ear stories about his gambling days with Grandfather:

'Your grandfather and I used to play cards together till three in the morning and then commandeer a donkey to get home. One night, sweet-up an' full of rum, we staggered out to climb on the donkey. We rode all night clinging on to each other. When de sun rose we find the donkey is tethered to a post going round in circles. Tee hee hee.'

Grandmother hastily extricated me from his company and instructed me to pass around a dish of canapes.

By four o'clock in the afternoon the funeral tea was over and the guests had vanished.

*

An hour or so later my parents had packed and were ready to leave. They were flying back to England that night while I was to stay on with my grandmother for the remainder of the school holidays. I waved them off in their taxi, a little apprehensive about being left on my own with my grandmother and aunt.

At seven in the evening Aunt Selma appeared downstairs dressed to the nines. She was wearing flowing voluminous robes in orange and black and a matching orange striped head-wrap with silver threads. Her hair was swept under the wrap to reveal dangling silver earrings and a heavy pendant around her neck. Her hands and wrists were weighed down with silver rings and bangles. She sailed like a galleon into the front room and went to pick up the telephone.

'And where de hell you think you goin' on the day of your father's funeral?' demanded Grandmother before Selma could dial a number. 'You can't go out dressed up like that today of all days.'

'Why not, Mother? You always told us he was an asshole,' said Selma calmly.

'What are people going to think if they see the Van Eysen girl out on the town the night her father was buried?'

'Mother, have you any idea what important event it is that I am attending?'

'I don't care what the hell it is. Yuh not goin'.'

Selma raised her voice just enough to overpower her mother's. 'I am going to see the Opera Flambeau. They are on tour and are only performing here at the Cultural Centre for one night. And do you know who is singing?'

'I don't give a toss who is singing.'

'Antonio Velasquez.' Selma hissed the name with great emphasis as if the mere sound of it would put an end to the argument. 'One of the best tenors ever to visit this country. One of the best tenors in the world.'

'You're a disgrace.'

'Well I'm goin'. I ain' missing one of the few international events that ever comes to this country just because father chose to bury himself on the wrong day. The whole country has been arguing about whether or not Velasquez is as good as Pavarotti.'

'How they know that if they've never seen him?' Grandmother's voice was deepening with rage. 'And they've never seen Pavarotti either.'

Selma pulled herself up to her full height. Her bosom swelled with indignation.

'I will tell you how we know, Mother. We read the reviews sent down from New York and from London and we take our sides from those! That is how we form our opinions in this country. We never get a chance to see these things so we read the reviews and take sides.'

Selma looked at her watch and dialled a number:

'This is Miss Van Eysen. Where de taxi? I ordered it for seven,' she snapped.

'You're not going. I can't stand it. I can't stand it. Oh God, why did you have to give me this pig-headed daughter?'

Grandmother rushed out of the room. Selma stood silently like one of the three Fates waiting for her taxi. Grandmother re-appeared smoking a cigarette and stood in the doorway blocking her exit:

'Well, I shall take de opportunity while you are out to tell both Pansy and Mohammed that they are no longer wanted. They're fired from this minute.'

At this news, Selma went rigid. Her lips clenched. Suddenly, she spun on her heel, tore off her head-wrap, flung it on the floor and glared with fury at her mother. Then she screamed:

'Don't you dare, Mother. Don't you dare. Those people have been with us for all my life since I was a child. I love them. An' you jus' goin' an' throw dem out like garbage? I won't hear of it.'

'Well, you can blasted well find the money to pay fuh dem,' countered my Grandmother.

'I will. I will do just that. I will do exactly that,' yelled Selma, kicking her head-wrap out of the way and charging out of the drawing room, slamming the door behind her. As she progressed to the far reaches of the house we could hear the sound of doors slamming with ever decreasing volume. There was silence. The taxi arrived, waited for a while then left again. Grandmother turned to me apologetically.

'There really is very little cultural activity here. You have to seize what you can when it comes. Excuse me while I go an' lie down for a little. I'm very tired.' She stubbed out her cigarette and went wearily up the stairs, leaving me on my own.

A while later Selma appeared in the doorway in a state of high agitation. Still dressed for the opera she tugged a black silk stole round her shoulders. Her hair was dishevelled, strands coming loose from the iron grey bun on top of her head. There were tears in her eyes. She brushed past me as if I didn't exist and went over to the mahogany bureau, opening each drawer in turn and rifling through papers and documents. Her lips were pursed as she chucked numerous letters, bills, papers, blotters and staplers into a heap onto the floor. Rummaging through the drawers she finally came across what she wanted: a sheaf of yellowing documents wrapped in red ribbon with something hand-written in copperplate on the front page and a red wax seal stamped on it. She shoved these in a cloth bag with zig-zag designs which she slung over her shoulder and went to the telephone:

'This is Miss Van Eysen. Can I have a taxi please to take me to the Rivoli Hotel.'

Her fat cheeks and lips quivered with emotion. She hurried to the cupboard where the housekeeping money was kept and helped herself to a roll of money. Then she left without saying another word. I watched her make her way to the waiting taxi, swatting away a marabunta hornet as she passed the allamanda bush. The last I saw of her were her silver sandals glinting in the moonlight.

What occurred at the Rivoli Hotel that night I heard later from Caso. Caso, Grandfather's old gambling buddy, had gone straight from the funeral tea to the Rivoli where he regularly staked his bets. He had witnessed all the events of the evening.

The Rivoli Hotel is a large dilapidated hotel on the Highway and the only hotel in Georgetown to contain a casino. The casino's clientele consists mainly of businessmen, some of whom recognised Selma as she entered and exchanged knowing glances with each other. Also gathered there were the usual riff-raff and desperados who haunt the gambling dens of any major city. Selma's appearance there caused quite a stir.

She elbowed her way through the crush, looking neither to left nor right and settled down immediately at the roulette table. There was a glint of determination in her eyes as she pulled her black silk stole round her shoulders. Her bracelets and bangles shone in the overhead light as she dipped into her bag and brought out the roll of dollars.

'Faites le jeu. Faites le jeu.'

She started modestly and placed a few thousand dollars on the red.

'Rien ne va plus.'

The wheel spun. She won and doubled her stake. She won again. A delighted Selma laughed and joked with some ruffian sitting next to her with whom she would never normally have exchanged a word. She won again. She fished in her bag and put another thirty thousand dollars on the red. Small beads of perspiration appeared on her upper lip as she focused on the spinning wheel. Under the table her foot was joggling with excitement. She continued to bet on the red long after most people would have heeded caution and changed their bets to black, thinking it impossible for the run on red to continue. But her number came up again. She grew increasingly confident and expansive, calling out merrily to people she didn't know on the other side of the table. She threw up her hands and made cooing noises of pleasurable surprise when the ball tumbled into the right slot. As often happens, the other gamblers recognised that someone was having a run of luck and crowded around her placing their bets alongside hers.

And win she did. Within an hour of sitting down at the table Selma had won enough money to keep Pansy the cook and Mohammed the night watchman in employment for the rest of the year. She scooped up her winnings, grabbed her bag and made to leave smiling around at everybody.

'That's it. Get out now girl. Get out now or yuh money goin' go like butter 'gainst de sun,' advised a bystander. People were patting her on the shoulder and congratulating her as she made her way out. Her bag with its zig-zag pattern was stuffed with dollars. She remained unaware of some people's disapproving glances and whispers about the woman who had come from her father's funeral to gamble.

A short man with greasy black hair and a cinnamon complexion grabbed Selma by the arm as she made her way out. His grip tightened. His eyes gleamed with malicious humour:

'Run from coffin an' yuh buck up wid jumbie,' he warned.

'Excuse me, sir.' Selma's voice rose in anger. Her large breasts were heaving: 'What is that stupidness? Yuh head ain' good or what?' She shook him off and headed for the door.

'Every stupit man gat 'e own sense.' The man shouted after her. Selma shook her head in impatient dismissal and disappeared into the crowd.

But just before she got to the swing doors at the front of the hotel Selma stopped. It was nine-thirty at night. There was time for another flutter. Why not? She walked back to the salon, hesitated, then instead of heading for the roulette tables she turned and made for the side room, where they played the card game Rouge et Noir, also known as Trente et Quarante. Rouge et Noir played for much higher stakes than was permissible when playing roulette. The roulette tables closed at midnight. Rouge et Noir could be played until three in the morning.

The side room where the game was being played was a good deal smaller than the open area that housed the roulette tables. A haze of cigar smoke hung in the air. Taking her seat at the card table Selma found herself surrounded by some dozen serious gamblers. She put down a substantial bet, her heart beating fast. The croupier was shuffling the six decks. He laid the cards out in two rows. Selma lost heavily and sucked her teeth, whispering imprecations under her breath. She placed another stake, lost again and sat the next game out. The confidence she had felt at the roulette table began to seep away. In a fit of peevishness and not wishing to look as if she were short of funds, she thrust all of her roulette winnings onto the table. Within an hour of sitting down at the table she had lost everything.

Stunned and feeling slightly sick, Selma pushed her chair back and fanned herself with a hotel brochure. The croupier on her side of the table offered her a blank card to cut the pack for the next game:

'Do you want to raise your stakes, Miss Van Eysen?'

Who knows whether it was embarrassment or a sudden craving for risk that made Selma reach in her bag and pull out the deeds of the house:

'Will you accept these?'

The croupier took them and checked with the supervising croupier on the other side of the table. He nodded:

'We put a price of two million dollars on the deeds. That is our limit.'

Selma looked a little startled then cast her eyes around at the other gamblers who were looking at her with curiosity.

'Go ahead,' she said and giggled.

They played on. She lost and watched in disbelief as the deeds of her house were passed to the winner, a well-built black man with rimless glasses whom she had never seen before.

According to Caso, an argument then ensued. Aunt Selma could not believe that she would not be given the deeds back. Surely, nobody could believe that anyone would seriously bet their house on the turn of a pack of cards. No. No. No. How could anyone think she was serious? It was just a game. In her mind it had no greater consequences than Snakes and Ladders. Selma's voice was raised to full volume. She stamped her foot and yelled. Security was called and she was escorted out of the salon.

Selma stood in the hotel foyer, bewildered. Then came the ice-bath shock of loss and with it the realization of what it all meant.

Meanwhile, at home I was reading in the living room when Grandmother wandered down and discovered the contents of the bureau strewn over the floor.

'Wha' happen' here?'

I explained that Aunt Selma had been looking for something in the bureau.

'Why she mek all dis mess? She still sulkin' in her room, I suppose.'

'No. She's gone out. I think she took a taxi to the Rivoli hotel.'

Grandmother stared at me. 'The Rivoli? Are you sure?'

'I think so.'

'Oh God. Oh God. Then you must go and fetch her back jus' now. She gone to the casino.' Grandmother looked distraught. 'Selma is very own-way an' sometimish. She very warrish when she wants. You mus' go. I can't go. I can't go there when I jus' bury my husband. You know how in Guyana people does know your business and spread it around. You mus' go. I will give you money for a taxi.'

She rushed upstairs to find her purse. I followed her to get my jacket. And then, for some reason, I came across Grandfather's black silk opera hat folded down in my suitcase and snatched it up. I was fifteen. I thought it would be a joke to take it with me.

Before I knew where I was Grandmother was pushing me out of the door towards a waiting taxi:

21

'Suppose they don't let me in. I'm not eighteen yet.'

'Yuh big an' tall like yuh grandfather. Tell them yuh eighteen. Look, yuh nearly have a moustache.'

I was half way down the drive when Grandmother called me back:

'Guilford. Wait. Ah comin'. I caan' let you go to that place on your own but I will not go inside the Rivoli. I will wait in the taxi outside while you fetch Selma. She might not want to come but you must persuade her, however long it takes. I will be waitin' in the taxi outside.'

She took a last draw on her cigarette and flung the glowing stub away behind her before taking me by the arm and hurrying with me towards the waiting cab.

The Rivoli is set some fifty yards back from the Highway. A random selection of lighted hotel windows blazed in the dark. The taxi dropped me off at the gate. Grandmother ordered the driver to move further down the road and wait there so that she could remain as far out of sight as possible.

I walked along the narrow paved path that led to the illuminated hotel entrance. It was a bright moonlit night and overhead Orion straddled the horizon but at a different angle from the one he occupies in the London sky. I sought out and found the two bright stars of the frog's eyes in the neighbouring constellation. They somehow reassured me. And in my jacket pocket I still had the Crown and Anchor dice Grandmother had given me at the funeral. I fingered them hoping they would bring me luck.

It seemed that the water feature just outside the hotel entrance had broken and was flooding the pathway. As I approached, I saw the figure of my aunt Selma come stumbling through the swing doors. She was clinging on to her bag. Her face was grey and I could see the pock-marks on her pouchy cheeks where she had once had chicken-pox as a child. Her steel-grey hair had come loose. Two dark circles under the armpits of her dress showed that she was perspiring heavily. She made no attempt to avoid the flowing water around her feet and staring straight ahead splashed right through it, soaking the bottom of her skirts.

I flicked open the black silk opera hat and put it on, waving at her so she would recognise me.

Selma stopped in her tracks. I could see her peering at me in the moonlight. Her hand shot up to cover her mouth. She gave a little whimper, looked away and looked at me again as I came towards her. Then, she raised her arms as if to ward me off and staggering slightly, she turned and splashed her way back into the hotel. By the time I got there she had collapsed in the foyer and was lying on the floor unconscious surrounded by people trying to minister to her.

'I think she took a stroke.'

The hotel management were fussing around and someone called for a doctor. The next thing I knew little wizened Caso was at my side.

'Yuh lookin' like yuh grampa. Is life in death she see when she look at you. Tek off de hat.'

He looked grim as he told me what had happened.

'Your aunt lose de house.'

I barely understood what he was saying. Aunt Selma seemed to be coming round. Someone had administered brandy. She was sitting up groggily leaning against a pillar.

'What should I do? We must get her to hospital. My grand-mother is outside waiting in a taxi.'

Caso turned to me.

'Listen to me nuh. Don' tell yuh granny nuttin'. It will kill her. I think your aunty goin' be ok. But dere is no way any of yuh could get nuff money to buy back de house. Yuh mus' get in there and try win it back. Is what yuh grandfather would do. Time for you to become a big man now. I will stay wid your aunt. Go now. Yuh ain'gat nothin' to lose.'

He explained to me roughly the rules of Rouge et Noir and gave me a shove towards the door:

'The deeds is a sheaf of papers. Someone will be holdin' on to dem. Yuh gat money? Yuh might as well try. Yuh can't get back de house no other way.'

I had the few thousand dollars Grandmother had given me for the taxi. At the door of the salon they enquired about my age.

'Eighteen,' I replied and was shown into the small room.

A large overhead lamp hung above the green baize card table. I had no idea what I was doing but I could see the deeds were now in the possession of a plump Indian woman with crimson lipstick. They must have changed hands several times adding a certain frisson to the game that evening. The rules were simple. All I had to do was choose between staking on the red or the black. I couldn't decide, red or black. Then I remembered the little golden frog I'd seen squatting on the hearts sign and I plumped for the red. The game began. At first my mouth went dry as black cards appeared everywhere like sinister sentries. The six of clubs prevented any progress. Unless some red card showed up, I'd had it. And then, suddenly, luck started clinging to the red. Everything upturned was red. First of all diamonds. Then hearts. Soft plush hearts. The world folded smoothly into order. The universe was in place.

Triumphant, I left the salon with the deeds grasped firmly in my hands. Caso stood in the foyer with my aunt Selma.

'Tee hee.' Caso clapped and gave a wheezy cheer when he saw me. 'Yuh done good. Yuh grampa watchin' over yuh. Yuh come Master of Chaos like he say.' He looked at his watch. 'Tek yuh Auntie Selma home. I jus' got time for a little Blackjack.' He seemed genuinely pleased at our good luck and handed Selma over to me before scuttling away.

Selma held on to my arm and remained silent. There was no doubting my feelings at the time. I felt I had undergone a rite of passage and become a man. I led my aunt down the path and guided her to where Grandmother waited in the taxi. Another tropical storm was threatening. Lightning put down its flickering white roots in the sky. Thunder rumbled in the distance. Nothing could dampen my elation. I was now an adult, grown-up and responsible for my aunt. In my hand I held the deeds of the house. I experienced an extraordinary feeling of euphoria. I had put the world to rights, re-established order and balance. I was Phaeton having regained mastery of the sun's chariot as it careered, out of control, across the sky.

In the taxi, with great pride, I handed back the deeds of the house to my grandmother. Neither of the two women spoke as the cab raced down the Highway. Grandmother said nothing but cast me a look of enormous gratitude.

Two streets from home we found fire engines blocking the road. Firemen denied the taxi entrance so we paid the driver off and walked round the corner stepping over the thick rubber hoses that snaked along the street. Nothing could have prepared us for the sight in front of us. Our house was engulfed in flames. Fire had reached the top of the roof and burst into a white fireball with a ragged yellow edge of flames which danced like yellow sea-horses. I remember my grandmother's screams as we clung on to one another although I barely remember what else happened in the next few hours. A neighbour gave us shelter that night. None of us slept.

The next morning we returned to the site. In front of us, still in a haze of smoke, stood the grey smouldering ruin of the house.

When I finally returned to my parents in England, I tried to give them an account of what had happened. No-one had been able to discover how the fire started. It could have been caused by lightning or by the cigarette stub which Grandmother had casually thrown away as we left home for the Rivoli, or maybe by some electrical fault. My parents comforted me as best they could after such a trauma. I thought a good deal about the words Grandfather uttered the night we sheltered under his umbrella waiting for the bus to Lewisham: 'Chance is random. Fate is not. Fate has a plan and fate wins in the end. But chance allows you to think you are escaping fate for a little while. Look. Here come de bus. We in luck.'

FABLE OF A LAUREATE

On the morning of his fateful decision, Noel Dunham was peering through the telescope he kept in the window of his study. His house perched on the Cornish cliffs near Lamorna Cove. Below him, a few holiday-makers could be seen walking along a cliff path. A thick sea-mist had rolled over Mount's Bay, blotting out the horizon and obscuring his view of the Lizard Point peninsula. It might well have been this disappearance of a familiar landmark, this vanishing into the mist and dissolution into nothingness that prompted the idea. For that was the day, Noel Dunham decided, that he was going to kill himself.

Six years earlier Noel Dunham had been awarded the Nobel Prize for Literature. He'd enjoyed the success, the travelling to speak at international literary festivals, the newspaper interviews, the television appearances, all of which had occupied him fully over a number of years. The problem was that ever since his trip to Sweden he had been unable to write a word. Whenever he sat down to start a new piece of work, he was paralysed by the fear that nothing he wrote would ever be as good as the work he had already created. A lifetime of working to a disciplined schedule meant that he continued to sit at his desk every morning. To no avail. He still worked, or tried to work, on an ancient typewriter. At the age of seventy-five he felt unable to adapt to new technology. But now he had begun to believe that his typewriter had a life of its own and was nursing malign intentions towards him. It squatted in front of him like a dangerous black insect. Whereas most things about Noel Dunham were well-worn and comfortable – his sagging face and rheumy blue eyes, the silvery pointed beard, his corduroy trousers – the typewriter facing him on the desk looked spiky and malevolent. Once, when he began to type, the keys all rose up at once like the swirling, clattering iron skirts of a furious Dickensian housekeeper and made him start back in fright.

His housekeeper in real life, Mrs Edwards, was the benign and friendly opposite of this threatening machine. She was enormously overweight. The fatness of her cheeks pushed her eyes up into a permanent slant. Her husband owned the best dairy in Penzance and she helped him to run it, while continuing to clean for Mr Dunham because she had worked for him before she married and did not like to let him down.

As Noel Dunham looked through his telescope at the heaving swell of the sea below and the eddying shapes of mist outside his window, Mrs Edwards pushed open the study door and entered the room sideways with his elevenses on a tray.

He put down the telescope and turned towards her.

'Mrs Edwards—' He hesitated, overcome with a sudden need to unburden himself. 'I am having some trouble with my work. I've got a little stuck.'

Mrs Edwards gazed at him, appalled . She had noticed for some time now that there had been no lively tap-dancing of the typewriter over her head as she cleaned and dusted downstairs. But she kept her counsel. It was no business of hers. All the same, somewhere in her mind she had always dreaded the day when something would be expected of her from this distinguished figure that she would be unable to deliver. That day, it seemed, had arrived.

'Oh dear,' she said. Her troubled breast rose and fell. Her mouth puckered and her weight caused her to pant a little as she spoke. 'Oh dear,' she repeated, then turned and left the room.

He knew immediately that he had breached some unspoken rule of etiquette between them. From upstairs he could hear Mrs Edwards speaking on her mobile phone.

'Why couldn't he ask me about milk-churns or ice-cream?' she was saying indignantly. 'Or butter-pats. Home-made cheese in muslin. Clotted cream or *something* I could help him with.'

Disappointed with himself for involving her in his dilemma, Noel Dunham, with great clarity of purpose, took some headed paper from the drawer, wound it into the typewriter and settled down to compose a suicide note.

'To whom it may concern . . .' That sounded a bit formal. Too legalistic and impersonal. He screwed up the paper and tossed it in the wastepaper basket. 'Life has become an intolerable burden.' Jesus Christ, he muttered to himself, how banal. I'm a Nobel prize-winner. I should be able to knock up a decent suicide note. He sprang up and went over to his bookcase. What kind of note did Ernest Hemingway write? He thumbed through one or two biographies. No mention of a suicide note. How inconsiderate. Novelists Yasunari Kawabata and H. Martinson the Swedish poet, were two other Nobel suicides who had neglected to write farewell notes. Infuriating. Well, what about Sylvia Plath? She wasn't a Nobel winner but what did she say? He approved of the brevity of Sylvia Plath's note: 'Call Dr Horder'. Succinct and practical. But she had already written it. He wouldn't like to be accused of plagiarism. The same went for Virginia Woolf. She had written a beautifully expressed suicide letter with not one jot of consideration for those who were to come after and might have liked to have written something similar themselves.

The old typewriter faced him like an implacable enemy, a metal gin-trap waiting to snap shut on his fingers. He gingerly inserted another piece of paper and tapped out a few words. 'Barometer plummeting. Stormy weather.' Too Ella Fitzgerald. He tore the paper out and flung it across the room. He considered doing something witty like leaving a full stop in the middle of a blank page. But people might not notice it.

Noel Dunham then decided to pull himself together and tackle the problem methodically. He would write every type of suicide note in every possible style and then go through them all until only one striking and inevitable farewell remained. For the rest of the morning he wrote an avalanche of suicide notes: magical realist suicide notes, a long epic suicide note, a brutal realist goodbye, a children's fiction suicide note, a series of post-modern adieus, an epigrammatic farewell, a suicidal limerick, a Haiku cheerio. They fell off his desk one after the other and began to pile up on the floor. The sun came out and dispelled the morning mists. He bent down and read everything he had written. After a while he groaned out loud and threw it all into the wastepaper basket. Nothing worked. He put his head in his hands. Like Prometheus he would be forced to continue living with his innards being constantly and

30

agonisingly gnawed by his inability to write a good enough suicide note.

At that moment Mrs Edwards appeared at the door. She was flushed. It was one of their unspoken rules that she did not come into his study again after she had brought his elevenses. Normally she would just finish her work and leave. But she felt that something untoward had happened. The rules had been broken. Some sort of chaos had entered the household. And she wanted to make amends for not being able to help him out of his impasse. For once she thought she would defy their code of conduct and say goodbye.

'I'm just going to fly off,' she said. 'I'm away now.'

Noel Dunham turned and looked at her in surprise. Slowly an expression of delight spread over the writer's face.

'Goodbye, Mrs Edwards. Thank you.'

He put a fresh piece of paper in the typewriter. He typed out the words: 'I'm just going to fly off. I'm away now.'

That would do. Simple. Direct. Touching on the poetic. Minimally humorous. The problem was solved.

He picked up his pen to sign his name. It occurred to him then that other Nobel laureates had been blessed with much more interesting and dramatic names than his own: Gabriel Garcia Marquez. Yasunari Kawabata. Svetlana Alexievich. Kazuo Ishiguro. Olga Tokarczuk. How dull the name Noel Dunham sounded in comparison.

His pen hovered over the paper but seemed unable to make contact with it.

REASON HAS ITS LIMITS

Of the five of us seated around a low table playing cards, I was the only one in civilian clothes. The other four were in military uniform. Whatever bad judgement had brought me there, I could see no immediate way of extricating myself. The room was austere and showed no hint of luxury. On one wall hung the official photograph of the bearded Colonel, now head of state, wearing his military beret with the badge in front. The single storey wooden house where we sat was situated some hundred yards from a sluggish creek that feeds into the Palumeu River. Outside, palm trees stood sentinel along the length of the creek, forming sharp black cut-outs against an evening sky streaked with pink and pistachio green. The sergeant dealing the cards wore the collar of his scruffy uniform unbuttoned. A damp cigarette hung from his lips as he collected the cards up from the table.

The Colonel leaned back in his chair with folded arms and waited for his hand to be dealt. He wore his familiar fatigues and boots. It is a dictator's duty to get up in the morning and make sure he looks exactly the same as the day before. There were tiny maggoty grey curls at the bottom of his beard. Some years after independence, the Colonel had led a military coup. He had elevated himself overnight from army sports instructor to Commander-in-Chief and head of state. 'Colonel Do' was how he liked to be known. He disliked intellectuals and considered himself a man of action. So they called him Colonel Do, or Do-Man or sometimes even Dr Do. At one point, under international pressure, the Colonel had been forced to give up his position and step aside but that was only temporary and with the now infamous 'telephone coup' he had stepped back into power again. Since then a court in The Hague had convicted him in his absence of narcotics offences and fraud and sentenced him to a term of imprisonment. Consequently, he was reluctant to travel abroad. He grew more reclusive and spent swathes of time in his retreat, fishing and playing cards but keeping an eye on the various militias in the bush who were mobilising against him. We had been there for two weeks. Boredom was setting in. Apart from the chirping of tree frogs outside, there was no sound except the shuffling of the pack, the slapping down of cards and the occasional groan from a player who had been dealt a bad hand.

How did I become so intimately involved with the Colonel? Well, I was working as a civil servant in the Ministry of Finance. The coup did not have much effect on our working lives. We just carried on as usual. Then one day the Colonel asked for someone from the ministry to come and help him deal with some matters regarding his personal finances. We all laughed in the office and joked about how we would have to teach him his two-times table. For some reason I was the one chosen to go.

I must say I was a little apprehensive when I entered the white colonial presidential palace. All sorts of stories had grown up around the Colonel during the civil war. It was said that once a skinny man wearing only camouflage army pants and a pair of sandals had come running out of the bush towards him brandishing in his right hand the three-inch-long purple finger of a dead man. Gasping for breath, he had offered it to the Colonel.

'We will win,' he said. 'This finger can make you invisible to the enemy whenever you need to be invisible. A djukka gave it to me.' He gave the trophy to the Colonel and ran back along the rough track road into the bush. The Colonel was said to keep this memento somewhere on his person and his rumoured ability to become invisible at will was one of the factors which demoralised his opponents.

However, there was nothing insubstantial about the man when I met him in his office. Wearing his standard military uniform, the Colonel stepped out from behind an enormous desk and held out a hand. To my surprise he was quite jocular. He was a burly man with a cast in one eye that made him seem almost humorous. Although he was clearly uneducated and spoke mainly in Sranen Tongo, there was no sign of the man whose reputation was for brutality and graft. He enquired about my background. I explained that my family came originally from Surabaya, Indonesia and that I had obtained a good degree in economics from Leiden University in The Hague. For a moment I thought I saw a shadow of dislike on his face but we chatted on quite amicably. Before long I found myself being taken into his confidence as he stared out of the window. I was faced with a request. Would I mind altering some documents and removing his name from them? He had enemies and did not wish to reveal to them the true origin of his finances lest they try to tap the same source. I have to admit to being craven in those circumstances. I did not like to imagine what would happen to me if I refused. Anyway, it seemed a harmless enough thing to do and I agreed. We shook hands. Back at the office I altered the documents without telling anyone. I gave him copies and thought no more of it.

But within days I was whisked out of my job in the ministry and appointed by the Colonel to be his personal aide. In that way he kept me close by his side. I was trapped. There were other things he asked me to do – falsification of diamond mine ownership and other forgeries. During the brief period when he was out of power I made every attempt to leave the country but his second coup came too quickly and dashed my hopes. I was back by his side wishing I were anywhere else.

The Colonel was smiling as he picked up his cards and addressed me with a chuckle:

'And so, Budi, what did you think of our telephone coup? One of my boys just picked up the telephone and said to the president: "Go home". It was as simple as that. The president picked up his papers and left. One telephone call and the government vaporised.'

'Oh, very good. Excellent,' I said, hoping to conceal my nervousness with a laugh. The strain of the last few months had caused itching hives to blossom on my neck and inner thighs.

Before his sentencing at The Hague, and while he was still able to travel, I had been co-opted by the Colonel to accompany him to one of the Caribbean islands. He went there to attend the gangster funeral of a top-ranking drug Don, a Don Gorgon who had funded projects throughout the region, including in Suriname. As usual, I was expected to tag along. In the blistering heat we followed the funeral cortege as it jerked its way down the unmade road from a twenty-bedroom palace at the top of the hill. The Don jolted along in his glass coffin like a black Snow White. The funeral was attended by major politicians whom the gangster had supported to the tune of several million dollars.

The Colonel had particularly admired the deceased because he'd emerged from a shanty-town and kick-started his career by going out and shooting fifteen people at random to show how useful he could be. He had grown rich enough to own an airline whose offices were housed in a tall multi-storey building of white purity which rose up high against the blue sky. On the outskirts of the city, scavengers could see the building from the massive garbage dump where they sifted and sorted their way through variegated mounds of refuse and waste packaging and from where, in nearby wooden shacks with no electricity, children emerged in beautifully pressed, pristine white shirts and blouses, making their way past the garbage to school.

'In this country we have to go to the drug barons and gangsters to ask for money to build a bridge or a road. Even the church pays for protection,' whispered one of the politicians as we traipsed along behind the cortege, our feet scrunching on the gritted path.

Soon after we returned to Suriname the judges in The Hague condemned and sentenced the Colonel in his absence, but Europe felt far away.

The game finished. The sergeant had won. He smiled but his eyes were loose and unsafe as he opened another bottle of Black Cat rum and poured some out for everyone. We had been drinking all afternoon. I leaned forward and brought out a suitcase full of euro notes from under the table, preparing to make the pay-out. The Colonel always insisted on using euros rather than Surinamese dollars. He was not a good loser. I tried to placate him by striking the right balance of familiarity and obsequiousness as I spoke, hoping to distract him from his defeat:

'So Do-Man, put us straight now that you are a world statesman. What will be the final struggle? China versus America? America versus Russia? Russia versus China?'

The Colonel's laugh rumbled directly from his stomach.

'No. No. No. None of those. The final struggle will be black against white.'

I was the only person there not of mainly African descent. My Indonesian ancestry meant that my face was smooth and yellow as a slab of toffee. I indicated my straight black hair with a coy gesture:

'So where does that leave the brown ones like me, Colonel? My family came here generations ago from Indonesia. Am I black?'

The Colonel lowered his eyes so that I would not see the contempt in them. I knew I had made a mistake. I was not sure what it was. We were used to any one of us falling out of favour for reasons we could not discern and becoming a scapegoat. He looked me up and down and then said with reluctance:

'In this instance, yes, you will count as black. The final struggle will be white against all the others. Those Marxist boys missed something. Race, religion and nationalism. Those are the things people are willing to die for.'

The Colonel swallowed another glass of rum, stood up and belched. He stretched, bent his knees like a weight-lifter and held his hands above his head as if grasping imaginary dumb-bells. Then he straightened up and strolled towards the window. Somewhere out there in the bush his former body-guard and rival commando Rudi Lichtveld was organising an insurgency against him with the support of the Dutch secret service. There was some sort of war over resources: diamonds; lumber; drugs and guns. The Colonel cast an eye over the guards who were keeping watch on his red and white seven-seater Cessna private aircraft perched on the airstrip outside. The white body of the plane was dazzlingly bright in the glare of the setting sun. Inside the cockpit, the pilot on standby dozed, his head drooping forward. The Colonel turned his back to the window and addressed me directly:

'You know what the sergeant here did to Rudi Lichtveld's lawyer when we found him?'

I shook my head.

'He cut the top joints of his fingers off with secateurs so that he would find it a bit more difficult to sign his legal documents.'

He gave a chuckle and waited to see my reaction.

'Good for him,' I murmured.

I glanced over at the sergeant whose unsettling dark eyes seemed to move independently as if they were in a pinball machine. He shrugged and reached for the rum bottle. There was an atmosphere of pent-up malignancy in the room which seemed to be waiting for some event or incident to release it.

The sun was sinking fast. One of the men went to switch on the generator and soon the room filled with anaemic blue light the colour of womb-water. The sergeant collected up the cards. All the military men were drunk now, the Colonel more drunk than anybody. He came towards me, swaying. It seemed I was to be the fall guy that day. He leered at me:

'You read books. If you're so clever tell me about Skrekibuku?'

I had heard of Skrekibuku, the shriek book, the book of terror, an ancient book of Dutch creole spells. Frankly, I despised that sort of superstition. I had been raised in the world of reason, mathematics and accountancy. He must have seen the dismissive expression on my face.

'You don't believe in that stuff, eh?'

From his top pocket he pulled the dead man's finger, now swimming in formaldehyde in a transparent plastic case, and waved it at me. Then he turned and clambered unsteadily onto the low card table fumbling in his holster to bring out his black Beretta handgun. His eyes were ranging round the four of us. We all knew what he was capable of in this sort of mood. I felt rivulets of cold sweat running down from my armpits. My hives began to itch unbearably.

Then out of the blue his humour changed and his face was festooned with smiles as he gazed at each one of us in turn. Without checking the safety catch, he grasped the barrel of the gun in his fist and turned the handle and trigger section towards his mouth as if it were a microphone. His other hand stretched out towards a vast imaginary audience. He shut his eyes and began to croon softly into the gun:

'Regrets, I've had a few
But then again too few to mention,
I did what I had to do
And saw it through without exemption.'

When he opened his eyes again they were glistening with tears.

'Yes, there were times, I'm sure you knew
When I bit off more than I could chew.'

The rest of us looked at him with fake smiles of admiration on our faces. It was difficult not to laugh. He swayed perilously close to the edge of the table. There was a pause as his head lolled forward and the hand holding the Beretta fell to his side. He raised his head and his eyes rolled as he struggled to stay upright. Then he brought the pistol-grip once more to his mouth and sang into it.

'I planned each charted course
Each careful step along the byway,
And more, much more than that
I did it my way . . .'

With a gesture, the Colonel commanded us to stand and join in. We rose uncomfortably to our feet and sang along with him. His voice rose.

'Yes, there were times, I'm sure you knew
When I bit off more than I could chew . . .'

He had forgotten the words but his face was still wreathed in smiles. The gun was waving around uncontrollably. In dark times it is important to remember your good manners. Fearing an accident and wanting to curry favour I scrambled onto the table to steady his hand. He pushed me away and tried to disentangle his hand from mine in such a clumsy way that the gun barrel twisted towards his face. Caught in the mechanism my finger involuntarily squeezed the trigger. There was a sharp sound like a twig snapping. The Colonel's body crashed on to me and I slipped off the table. We both fell to the floor. I lay there for a minute and then got up. The Colonel continued to lie there, a pool of blood spreading slow as black molasses on the wooden floor. The sergeant's jaw dropped as he looked at me with disbelief.

There is a saint who asks no questions. Our Lady of Death. Saint Death, I think they call her. She's Mexican or Aztec, something like that. You can ask her for anything and she will turn a blind eye. She makes no moral judgement so you can ask, 'Please help me kidnap this baby', or 'Please steady my hand as I plunge the knife in'. She's a good one to have on your side. Believe you me I'm not at all religious but at that moment I muttered to her, 'Please help me out of this situation.'

It must have worked. Fearing they would be accused of dereliction of duty in failing to protect him, the sergeant and the other bodyguards put their heads together and decided to say he had committed suicide. His prints would be all over the gun. My prints would be there only because I had tried unsuccessfully to stop him. We all shook hands in agreement.

Having settled on this story they ran outside to raise the alarm. The Colonel's body was carried to the seven-seater Cessna and bundled in. I climbed in next to the pilot. He was instructed to fly us both back to hospital in Paramaribo immediately. I expanded the suicide story to the pilot as we lifted off over the bush. Below I could see the sergeant and the rest of the bodyguard packing up to leave with the clear intention of defecting and going over to Rudi Lichtveld's side.

In the cramped space of the cockpit I glanced over my shoulder at the Colonel's body lying between the seats. Something had fallen from his pocket. I reached back to pick it up. It was the purple dead man's finger that was supposed to confer invisibility on the owner if needed. For some reason I did not want the pilot to see it, as if anything out of the ordinary might be a clue to my guilt. Irrational, I know. I shuffled round and hid it in my bag. The journey to Paramaribo airport took three-quarters of an hour. When we arrived an ambulance was waiting. Police were everywhere. In the confusion of the body being transferred from the plane to the ambulance I slipped away to an adjoining area of the airport.

I am not superstitious. I was brought up with all the benefits of the rational age of enlightenment but I walked through that airport without a passport, without being stopped or seemingly even noticed and boarded a plane for Amsterdam with no ticket. In Amsterdam's Schiphol airport an equally unlikely scenario occurred. The electronic passport control jammed. For a few moments, before a supervisor came and stopped them, flustered airport staff waved people through with no checks. The electronic gate was open. I passed with no hindrance and continued to the 'Nothing to Declare' exit without being stopped. In a daze I found myself walking through the air-conditioned shopping arcade, surrounded by glass-fronted stores with displays of luxury leather goods, perfumes, watches, jewels – even Surinamese diamonds – and electronic devices. Eventually, I stepped out into the night.

I still had in my possession the large bundle of euros from my role as banker in the card game. And so I took a taxi out into the snowy Amsterdam winter.

In the Prins café on Prinsengracht, I ate my favourite pastries and drank coffee. I paid and left. Outside I stepped into a hailstorm. I lowered my head against the driving white force of hailstones that rattled on the ground and swept the canal footpath like a yard brush. Standing by the canal railing, braced against the hail, I must have made an odd sight in my light tropical suit and panama hat. But nobody seemed to notice. I fished in my pocket and threw the container holding the dead man's finger into the icy grey waters of the canal.

Then I set off to look for a hotel.

FABLE OF A GOD FORGOTTEN

The wide empty corridors of the asylum were silent. At that time of day, an hour or so after lunch, the place was quiet. A solitary figure walked along the shiny brown linoleum floor of the corridor keeping always to the centre. On either side of him the evenly spaced office doors were closed. Inside each office, on the desk, was an alarm bell. He walked down the corridor towards the blank cream-painted brick wall at the end where a metal bucket full of water and detergent and a string mop had been left in the corner for him. Overhead, above the wall, a square glass skylight was set in the ceiling. When the patient reached the end of the corridor he stood there in the shaft of light, his face upturned towards the sun. After a while he picked up the mop and started to wash the floor, filling the air with the smell of disinfectant. This was a privilege he had earned.

Progress had been made. He had been moved from the stage where no-one was allowed within six feet of him. That was for the most dangerous. He had been kept at that stage for only ten days after his admission. A warder and a nurse would look through the spyhole of the cell door and ask him to stand at the back, beneath his window, as far away from the door as possible. Then they would open the door quickly and place his food, drink and medication just inside before retreating and locking the door again. He hardly posed a threat. The warders were mostly twice his size. It was security protocol.

After that came the stage when he had to be kept within eye contact. Never out of sight. That had been the position for the next year. There had been no psychotic episodes in that period although there had been one or two blips. Once it seems he had been impersonating a doctor and writing letters to find the whereabouts of his last victim. Another time a group of patients had signed a petition warning against his release on parole. They accused him of being involved in the death of another patient. But after many investigations nothing was ever proved. Now he was being re-assessed.

A psychologist looked through his reports to evaluate his suitability for temporary release. She flicked through a thick dossier of background notes. There was a small photograph of him stapled to the first page of the file.

Yes. He was a sad creature. Thinning fair hair. Broad forehead. Blue eyes. Dragged through children's homes and asylums. Desperately neglected. A poverty-stricken background somewhere in the north of the country. Possibly schizophrenic. A danger to women. Convictions for both rape and murder. Himself terribly abused in childhood. Ordered to be detained in a secure hospital. The psychiatrist's report showed the different medications prescribed since his arrival. Largactil mainly. The nurses' daily reports were handwritten in biro, each paragraph carefully dated and in different handwriting. Nothing exceptional in his behaviour. The occasional petty quarrel with another patient duly logged. Largely co-operative. Symptoms of schizophrenia no longer apparent.

Seven years after his admission he was considered eligible to be released on licence. 'Leave in the community' it was called. This was a trial for a week which, if successful, could lead to a more extended parole. It was approved and he was placed in a hostel.

It was the middle of the night. I do not know how he got in. Something woke me and in the dim light I saw the dark shape of a figure about four feet away in the doorway of my bedroom. It recoiled for a moment and then launched a savage attack. The eruption of violence felt as if it were enveloping me. I was pinioned by his weight to the bed. A gloved hand tore at my mouth. A rope was being pulled round my neck. A roar issued out of my throat. His voice was gruff and wheezy:

'Shut up. Shut up. Don't move. Don't move.'

I raised my head from the pillow, trying to avoid suffocation and fought back managing to untwist the sheet from my legs. There was a fierce struggle. With a huge effort I contrived to lift us both and get my feet on the floor. I stood up and some-how pulled the length of rope from around my neck. It dropped to the floor. He darted behind me. His bare muscular arm locked like a vice around my neck. I could feel the silky hairs on his arm. I tried to twist my head round towards him. The voice was a low growl:

'Don't look round. Don't look round.'

Some instinct told me not to look. My heart was beating fast. I was naked. I felt extraordinarily alive. A captured wild animal alert to everything around me. Waiting for my chance. I turned my head slightly to look for a weapon.

He growled again, 'Don't look round.'

That should have been a clue. A stirring of memory. Some-thing I had read about before. An ancient story. Someone else,

45

was it a pregnant woman, had insisted on seeing . . . on coming face to face . . . and been destroyed by the wild lightning shock and voltage of the confrontation.

I did not look round. I thought of biting the arm. The danger was that it would produce a more violent response from him. He was stronger than I was. I was trembling. All the same I lashed out, punching at his face over my shoulder. He grabbed my hand and bent the fingers back. I pulled the hand away. No weapon nearby that I could see. Stalemate. We stood there in the dark. Me in the arm-lock. Both of us out of breath. Panting after the fight. Deadlock. Unmoving.

And then for the most fleeting of moments I had a revelation and with it a flash of envy. How extraordinary to be so truly free. To exist outside the shackles which bind the ordinary law-abiding citizen. What liberation. To break every rule and slip the bonds of humanity. The incredible daring of it. To step out of all those restrictions and moral structures and let them just fall away around your feet. The shedding of morality. How enviable. To be nothing but what the forces of nature demand. Elemental. To shake off every restraint laid down by decency and the law, those reins and harnesses all undone, leaving only this energy, this electrifying presence, this shocking electro-magnetic force field. How bold. How admirable. For a minute, behind me, stood an incandescent god. A golden god from the time before religion and morality became entwined. So this is what it means to be divine. Super-powerful and sub-human at the same time, divine and bestial. I understood, for the briefest of moments, that he had drunk the milk of paradise.

It was a strange epiphany, lasting only a few seconds. One thing was certain. This god had nothing to do with love. More like Tlaloc the Aztec god with his lightning axe, or Zeus himself. Nor was there a sense of a god who wanted to be worshipped. No adoration required. Not even approval. He would have despised people falling to their knees. What he expected was simple. Just to be acknowledged. A recognition of his existence. Nothing more.

And then those seconds passed. My mind raced back to the immediacy of the situation, my head in an arm-lock. What were the possibilities of escape? Every sinew and muscle was tensed and ready for action. I started to bargain. The ordeal went on for two hours. The balance of power shifted from one to the other. He escaped before it became light outside. I survived.

After the trial and the guilty verdict his defence lawyer said:

'He is the most dangerous man I have ever come across in all my years at the bar.'

He was returned to the secure hospital.

Yes. He was a sad creature. Thinning fair hair. Broad forehead. Blue eyes. Yes. Terribly abused in childhood. Desperately neglected. Might be a paranoid schizophrenic but later they discovered that he was able to simulate those symptoms, able to assume the cloak of mental illness when it suited him. All the same, dragged through children's homes and asylums. Poorly educated but possessing a degree of natural cunning. Never properly cared for. Abandoned many times as a child. Surely deserving of care and nurture. Pitiable really.

Or a god forgotten.

THE DOSTOYEVSKY HOUSE

Nikolai Timurovich Pestov knelt on the arm of the old sofa with his left ear pressed to the partition wall. Dammit. It had happened again. How many times had he shown his neighbour the trick of flushing the toilet cistern so that it would not leak? The gurgling and groaning he could hear through the wall meant that soon a damp patch would appear behind the sofa in his living room.

The Petersburg flat was a communal one. Nikolai and his family shared a toilet and kitchen with two elderly neighbours, the Korsakovs, and Nikolai longed to find enough money to buy them out. His wife too was feeling the strain. That morning, when he went out to the shops, she had been playing the theme tune from *The Umbrellas of Cherbourg* on the piano, humming to herself with tears in her eyes which she hoped he would notice.

Nikolai detached himself from the wall and stood up. For a moment he confronted himself in the mirror, a fifty-two year old actor with floppy black hair and lop-sided features that gave his long face a naturally comic appearance. He wore only a grey vest t-shirt and some checked cotton shorts. His reflection told him nothing he did not already know and he crossed over to the table to inspect the food his wife had left out before she went to work: a large dish of cold soup made from beans and tiny cubes of cucumber, four slices each of salami and cheese and half a loaf of black bread. As he put the kettle on and sat down to eat, he heard the key in the front door. His thirteen-year-old daughter Sonya was back from school. She was an odd elfin creature with a crooked face, dark intense eyes and a determined selfishness about her that called to mind some of his older Tatar relatives in Kazan. Sonya walked past him swinging her satchel, went straight to her room, and slammed the door.

'Food's on the table,' he called.

No reply. He could hear the reedy sound of music from her headphones. He went to shut the front door which she had left ajar. Creeping across the shared lobby was Mr Korsakov who flashed Nikolai an obsequious smile before letting himself rapidly out.

He sat down again to eat. Next to his right hand was a rolled-up newspaper he kept to combat the plague of flying ants that had invaded Petersburg that summer. He was about to take a swipe at one or two of the pests flitting near his head when he spotted something in the small print of the newspaper. It was a notice from the European Union offering a substantial grant to Russian writers and illustrators for work that promoted moderation and tolerance in accordance with the values of the European Union. They had to send in applications. Nikolai read it with interest. He would show it to the small group of writers and artists whose meetings he attended whenever his work as an actor allowed.

At five thirty he shouted goodbye to Sonya, took his bicycle, and set off for the theatre. Tonight was the last night of an adaptation of Gogol's *The Nose*. Nikolai was playing The Nose. After that there would be no more income except from his wife's work as a canal-boat tour guide. The theatre was part of the building complex that housed the Dostoyevsky Museum. With the newspaper in his pocket Nikolai cycled along the canal paths in the warmth of the summer afternoon.

Standing in the doorway of the Dostoyevsky building, as Nikolai approached, was Pyotr Stepanovich, curator of the Dostoyevsky Museum and warden of several other apartments in the building – a plump, silver-haired man with a cherubic face and an expression of jovial disrespectful humour.

'Ah, my dear Kolya.' He bubbled over with impatience as Nikolai dismounted from his bicycle. 'Those idiots in apartment No. 7 have blocked the ventilator. I'm just having it fixed. They've always been pests. Last winter when the heating broke down they tore up all the parquet flooring and set fire to it.' Pyotr continued without pause: 'But what's worse is that some corporation wants to open up a chain of replica Dostoyevsky apartments all over town with underground skating rinks or car parks or something. They are frightened that another firm will poach me and they want me to sign a document saying I don't exist and that I've never existed.'

'Don't sign it,' said Nikolai. 'You'll do yourself out of a job. Have a look at this.' He pulled the newspaper out and showed the advertisement to Pyotr.

'Phew.' Pyotr raised his eyebrows and looked impressed. 'That's interesting. The group is meeting tomorrow night. Why don't you bring this along? The usual place, Vasili's apartment in Mokhovaya Street.'

Nikolai made his way into the theatre. His colleague Fyodor was already applying make-up in the cramped dressing room.

'I'll be glad to be doing this for the last time,' Nikolai said as the dresser strapped him into an enormous prosthetic nose, then helped him into the costume of a state councillor, plumed hat, gold-embroidered uniform and breeches.

As the play reached its climax a member of the audience shouted out to somebody across the auditorium: 'Oh for God's sake stop rustling those sweet-papers.'

A voice from the stalls shouted back: 'It's my birthday and I'll eat as many sweets as I want to.'

The actors continued stoically and took their final bows.

After the performance, Fyodor and Nikolai, friends since the days they had been brought from the provinces as pioneers to train as actors in Leningrad, went for a meal at a Ukrainian restaurant around the corner.

A sulky old man in the scarlet baggy trousers of Ukrainian national dress sat by the entrance.

'How is Ukraine?' Nikolai asked with concern.

The old man shrugged: 'It's all the same to me. I'm going back to Canada in two weeks' time. I live there now. I'm just dressed up like this to help my brother-in-law.'

The two actors pulled chairs up to a table under the window and ordered marinated herrings with boiled potatoes, some raw red onion rings and a beetroot salad. Nikolai tucked into his herrings:

'I still think the old ways were best, ensemble work with permanent companies.'

Fyodor shook his head:

'No, we got stale. Now we can experiment. Try new stuff. What's the matter with you, Nika? You didn't like communism, now you don't like capitalism.'

Nikolai grinned and banged his fist on the table: 'I'm

Russian. Nothing pleases me. Have you got any work coming up?'

'I have,' replied Fyodor. 'I'm working for an oligarch. He's making fake documentaries on the Ukraine for Russian television. All I needed was to be able to do a Ukrainian accent. Half of his estate has been made into a vast tank training ground scarred with caterpillar tracks. Tanks are hired and blown up. It's quite something.'

'What's his name?'

'I don't know. We all address him as Midas.'

Nikolai was impressed: an oligarch so elevated that he had no name.

Fyodor continued: 'He's intending to run for president. I expect he'll choose a name then. He seems quite friendly – comes down to watch the shoot and we chat. Apparently, his advisor has told him he needs to spend time in prison to boost his credentials as a dissident in opposition. I could probably get you a job working for him too.'

Nikolai pulled the newspaper from his pocket: 'Thanks, maybe, but I'll try this other little project first.' He showed Fyodor the advertisement.

'Good luck with that,' said Fyodor.

The friends finished their meal and waved each other an affectionate goodbye on the canal footpath.

Nikolai cycled along the embankment past the façades of the Italianate buildings. It was that time of year when the pale sun still shone late into the night. In the summer light the mustard yellows, dusky pinks and pistachio greens of the house fronts reminded him of the chalk pastels he had used as a child at school in Kazan. A boy sitting at the side of the road unfolded his accordion which suddenly burst into blossom with a Strauss waltz. Nikolai cycled on home, his spirits raised.

The Berlaymont building, headquarters of the European Commission in Brussels, rose up like a sparkling cliff against the blue sky.

A black limousine with tinted windows drew up in the fore-court, forcing a tiny old woman pushing a bicycle to give an eccentric cat-leap to one side to avoid being knocked down. Out of the car strode a short balding man bristling with purpose. Up the ramp he went at phenomenal speed and disappeared into the building.

A few minutes later Madame Ursula Schultz, a neatly coiffed, blonde woman in her forties, wearing a blue and white neckerchief, stood outside looking up at the glittering mega-block where she was due to attend a meeting about her next posting to Russia.

Once inside the building she was assigned an escort, a bright breezy young woman with long legs. Madame Schultz's stride was shorter. Her calves ached as they raced along the carpeted corridors. Just as the guide was telling her how easy it was to understand the layout of the building, a lift stopped beside them. The doors opened to reveal a group of people shouting and waving their arms:

'We are lost. Help us. We are lost. Which floor is the—' The lift doors shut and the lift continued on its downward journey.

The escort ushered her into the conference room and departed. Committee members were gathering. Madame Schultz found her name-card at the large oval table and sat down, placing her handbag carefully at her feet. In front of her a fixed microphone reared up like a single black spermatozoon on a thin curved stalk.

The Director of Commission, Mr Jan Jesek – the very same balding man who had catapulted out of the limousine – now appeared in the doorway. He sat down at one end of the table and leaned towards his microphone.

'Good morning to you all. As you know, our function here is to implement the decisions taken by the European Parliament. Parliament is anxious to rein in Russia after their behaviour in the Ukraine and to bring them round to our way of thinking. This has meant the imposition of sanctions and the cancellation of some of our Russian projects. Funding for the construction of the sludge incineration plant in Petersburg, for instance, has been withdrawn.

'However, Parliament believes that we can still influence Russia through culture. And the purpose of this meeting is to welcome Madame Schultz, who has left her posting in Brazil and is now the new Head of Co-operation in our Russian delegation in Moscow.'

A faint ripple of applause went round the table.

'Madame Schultz will be in charge of implementing the cultural co-operation project. With regard to Russia, we want to encourage and disseminate our values of tolerance, our sensitivity to ethnic differences and, above all, our respect for moderation. We in the European Union want to make the world a better place. So we will promote magazines and graphic works challenging extremism and the problems of corruption and xenophobia apparent in Russia today.

'The contract will fall under the Respect programme's outreach strategy for value-driven pedagogical tools. The grant will be put up for tender in the usual way and will be given to whichever group of Russians earns the approval of the Evaluation Committee. The European Union will contribute 80 per cent of the total – that is 70,000 euros – and the other 20 per cent must be raised by the Russians themselves. Madame Schultz, may we all wish you well.'

The meeting over, Mr Jesek gathered his belongings and left the room. The other committee members gradually dispersed.

Madame Ursula Schultz lingered to breathe in the air of her new responsibilities. It would be up to her to give a gentle tweak to the tail of the Russian bear and lead it in the direction of moderation and Western-style democracy. She rather wished now that she had not exaggerated the extent of her Russian speaking abilities on her CV. But she determined to remedy that with study and a new dictionary.

The next day she flew to Moscow.

Over the years a small group of writers and artists in Petersburg had built a nest in Vasili Babikov's second-floor apartment in Mokhovaya Street. They had started as the Rehabilitation of Obscure Poems Society. This flourished until a ferocious argument about the merits of a certain lyrical poet resulted in one of their number saying goodbye after dinner and throwing himself out of the tall casement windows onto the cobbles below. Since then the group had met, squabbled, read each other's work and submitted various stories and poems for publication in magazines – while always keeping the casement windows shut. They had been thus engaged for over thirty years.

The footpath along Mokhovaya Street consisted of mud baked hard by the heat with a few sparse shoots of grass poking through. Nikolai lifted the latch on a pair of heavy wooden doors with iron struts that led into Vasili's apartment building.

The badly-lit entrance lobby with its stone walls exuded a smell of damp and mould. Facing him was a circular stairway with wide pitted stone steps. Grey light filtered through the large dirty window on the first-floor landing opposite. A glass jar half full of cigarette ends stood on the window sill. He made his way up to the second floor.

He had, in fact, glimpsed Vasili Babikov a few weeks earlier. Nikolai had fallen asleep on the metro and overshot his stop. As he ascended the escalator he caught sight of Vasili, dressed as usual in black, like an undertaker, descending on the downward escalator:

'Oi. Vasili. I thought you'd retired.'

'No. Died,' came the response as Vasili, without looking up, was swept down to the depths of the station.

Nikolai rang the doorbell. Vasili opened the door and ushered him inside. Nikolai noted two silvery moths clinging to the lapel of Vasili's jacket. And this was a man who used to be immaculate and was even known, in his youth, to have made sure that a trouser press was available before getting in to bed with a new lover.

The apartment consisted of one large high-ceilinged room with casement windows and a small balcony. Opening off this room were four or five doors leading to quarters which the Babikovs let out to various lodgers. At the far end was a parrot in a cage covered by a green brocade cloth. The room contained an oval mahogany table surrounded by chairs and a small side table holding an electric samovar.

The core group of writers was already assembled. Shimon Simonov, a tall stooping ex-alcoholic who considered himself an expert on Pushkin, was seated next to Pyotr Stepanovich from the Dostoyevsky Museum. Egor Dudnik, a man with a bristling black moustache, who was easily brought to the point of seething, was standing near the table. Egor had a chip on his shoulder about his name. He was convinced that his name was only suitable for a village idiot. A talented cartoonist, he made his living carving tombstones. The cemetery business was booming, with the new middle class favouring black marble headstones. Every day, Egor Dudnik resented having to inscribe names more impressive than his own.

Nikolai and Vasili came to sit down at the table.

Just then a door at the back of the main room opened and in bustled Olga Stepanovich, Pyotr's wife, a plump rosy woman with a slight squint. Arms outstretched, she made a bee-line for Nikolai and embraced him.

'You. It is you who are to blame for all this happiness.' She planted a kiss on his cheek. 'Our entire lives are about to change.'

Her husband groaned. 'Where do you think you are, Olga, in a Chekhov play?'

'We will buy one of those Nespresso coffee machines,' she said, snatching her handbag from the table where she had left it earlier and heading for the back room again.

Two minutes later she re-emerged, this time without a smile and looking grim. She marched over to the front door of the apartment and turned the key in the lock so that no-one could leave.

'Excuse me. My watch is missing. I'm sure you won't mind if I just check your pockets to see if any of you picked it up by accident.'

With that she proceeded to frisk Nikolai, patting him down before turning to Shimon Simonov who meekly submitted to the search.

'I don't suppose you would stoop to taking your wife's watch but I'll check just the same.' She briefly inspected her husband's pockets before turning to Egor who already stood with his empty pockets turned inside out. Then, clucking with annoyance, she marched back to the other room. After a few minutes:

'Found it!' she shouted. She returned, smiling as before and headed for the exit. 'A Nespresso coffee machine like the one George Clooney advertises,' she reminded her husband before leaving.

After that interruption Vasili served everyone tea along with some stale blinis.

'I think we should get down to business,' he said.

The other members of the group gathered behind Pyotr Stepanovich to peer over his shoulder as he opened up his laptop and revealed the full text of the European Union project.

'We in the European Union want to make the world a better place,' read out Shimon Simenov in bewilderment, raising his arms to reveal the threadbare elbows of his jacket. 'And what makes them think they are qualified to adjust reality in such a way?'

Egor Dudnik butted in, all the energy seeming to gather in his moustache:

'Who do these foreigners think they are, anyway, coming over here to teach us about xenophobia? We have a long and glorious history of it without their interference. The next thing we know they'll be trying to re-write our great Russian novels to make them more moderate: *Crime and Punishment* – oh . . . Raskolnikov mustn't murder the old woman. Why doesn't he bring her some soup and bread rolls instead? *Anna Karenina* – oh how we cheered when she fell under the train and someone pulled her out just in time. I'm not at all sure we should be having anything to do with the European Union.'

'You may be right,' said Vasili looking glum. 'Corruption is part of our legacy: tsars, commissars, oligarchs, all fleecing us. What would we do without it? How would we create our wonderful literature with its starving masses and cabbage soup swimming with cockroaches?'

'I disagree. I think Russia belongs with Europe.' Nikolai turned to Pyotr. 'What would the English say if they were applying? They're beacons of moderation.'

'Oh, the English.' Pyotr pulled a face. 'They would say "Let's not kill the Queen. Let's give the poor some socks".'

This struck Nikolai and Pyotr as so hilarious that they doubled up with uncontrollable giggles.

Egor continued defiantly: 'Let the Europeans keep their J.K. Rowling – sitting on top of the bestseller list for years because she's too idle to get off. We have our own dragons, our own house goblins hiding in magic eggs, not to mention our talking cheeses of yesteryear.'

This made Nikolai and Pyotr laugh even more until Nikolai suddenly announced in all seriousness: 'I think Pushkin would have wanted Russia to join the E.U.'

There was a moment's silence before Egor Dudnik exploded: 'Pushkin? The father of Russian literature?'

There followed such a fierce argument about whether or not Pushkin would have wanted Russia to join the European Union that Vasili checked to make sure the casement windows were shut. Pyotr and Nikolai swore that Pushkin would have been in favour. Vasili and Egor argued that he would not. Finally, Shimon Simonov, alleged expert in all things Pushkin-esque, rose to his feet. Fearing that he was about to start reciting

The Bronze Horseman – which he often did as a prelude to his pronouncements and which took over twenty minutes – Vasili suddenly bellowed:

'Comrades!' surprising himself at the use of a term that had not passed his lips for thirty years. 'Please look at the amount of money involved here, 70,000 euros. After we have set aside money for printing and distribution and, of course, a sum for the treatment of our friend and founder member, Ivan Persikov's cancer, who would like to pocket several thousand euros?'

Shimon Simonov sat down again. Everyone round the table raised their hands.

'Then let us get on with the job of making our application,' continued Vasili. 'We need something interesting, but not too interesting, with a sizeable helping of blandness. Surely that is not beyond our talents.'

They set to work. Egor rushed home to fetch his draughtsman's table. The others sat with pen and paper. Soon something began to take shape.

It was decided at this point to bring in Mrs Babikov. Yelena Babikov, who swayed and waddled as she walked and had the vacant face of one prone to religious mania, had been the butt of such constant teasing and mockery all her life that she had become sensitive to the suffering of others and was tolerant and kind. She could be the arbiter of any material too cruel or extreme.

They all put pens to paper and under Yelena's direction came up with enough ideas for a moderate graphic anti-bigotry magazine that fulfilled the E.U. Commission requirements. At eleven o'clock that evening they were all agreed on the content and with a 'ping' it was submitted by email as required to the Evaluation Committee.

Vasili went to the drawer of the small side table and took out three bottles of vodka. Before long Nikolai had found some music and was executing a lively Georgian folk dance around the table. Vasili was standing on a chair with a flush to his melancholic pallor, making a toast to windmills.

'And I shall continue to tilt at windmills until I catch one of them off-guard,' he announced to cheers and applause.

The evening spun on into more toasts and much hilarity.

Around midnight when, at that time of year, the sun over Petersburg seems to set and rise in the same place, utterly confusing east with west, Vasili found some sparklers which they all lit and waved around.

As the sparklers went out the mood suddenly changed and they decided that life was not worth living and that they should go down to the River Neva and drown themselves. Nikolai, the more optimistic of the group, managed to dissuade them from this course of action and in the morning, under a sun which had never properly set, they were to be found sprawled over chairs and on the floor of Vasili Babikov's shabby apartment.

Madame Schultz's luxury apartment was situated in one of the most exclusive districts of Moscow. As with all postings in less reliable countries, a guard in a sort of sentry box on stilts was maintained by the E.U. just inside the metal grid gates of the compound. The guard concealed his three toddler children in the bottom of the dark box until, every morning, when Mrs Schultz's driver had taken her to work, the children were unleashed into the garden. Similarly, in the evening when he received a signal from a colleague that she was on her way back, the children were shovelled back in the box until the end of his evening shift.

Madame Schultz found herself, however, upon the horns of an intractable dilemma at the office. The E.U. Head of Delegation and Head of Commission, her boss in Moscow, and his counterpart, the Head of Commission in Brussels, were at war, refusing to speak to each other. The Head of Delegation in Moscow would only address emails to the secretary of his counterpart in Brussels. His counterpart refused to read any emails addressed to his secretary. This meant that the Evaluation Committee for her project was unable to make headway. She decided the only way forward was to break with E.U. protocol requiring all communication to be by email and to visit the groups who had applied, even the one in Petersburg, and check that they were bona fide groups of writers and artists. She interviewed the Moscow applicants first.

Most of these had fashionably short greased hair that stood up like iron filings under a magnet. Some had tattoos and a competitive glint in their eyes. They were the new entrepreneurs, graphic designers who worked for fast-food companies or had started up dog-grooming businesses. They had spotted the advertisement and cobbled together various proposals in order to win the grant. When Madame Schultz looked over the applications it was the one from Petersburg that seemed the most promising in its adherence to the values of the E.U. She sent them an email saying that they should arrange a date for her to visit.

On the day of the visit, the sun peeped through the casement windows into the Babikovs' freshly cleaned apartment. The literary group had assembled in good time, respectably dressed and with minds singularly focused on the proximity of the grant. They had taken a vow not to contradict Madame Schultz and to talk only in terms of moderation and tolerance. In the interests of gender equality, Mrs Yelena Babikov had been included in the company.

It was Madame Schultz's first visit inside a Russian household. She was introduced to them one by one – with Egor Dudnik going crimson as his name was mentioned. Her informality, friendliness and passable grasp of the Russian language soon allowed the group to relax.

'I thought your proposal for an anti-bigotry magazine was very interesting,' she said, 'and I've brought something to show you on my laptop to prove that the European Union also has soul, that it is not entirely focused on specifications for vacuum-cleaners or introducing the regulatory size for Europe-wide toilet cisterns.'

Nikolai Pestov could hardly believe his ears.

'Do you mean that you have regulated cisterns throughout the continent?' he enquired, immediately becoming even more enamoured of the European Union.

A little unsure of her ground, Madame Schultz said she thought so.

'Anyway,' interrupted Pyotr Stepanovich in an ingratiating tone of voice, 'we know that the E.U. has soul. They have a statue of Robert Schumann the composer outside their building.'

'Ah,' Madame Schultz was smiling. 'Many people make that mistake. That statue is of Robert Schuman, accountant and lawyer and founding father of the European Union. But let me show you what is on my laptop here.'

Pyotr cringed at his mistake. All the members of the group gathered obediently around her.

She switched on her laptop. There was a tinny rendition of Beethoven's 'Ode to Joy' and on to the screen sprang a square-jawed woman with solidly set blonde hair. She spoke with a barely suppressed hysteria that was evident even in the Russian sub-titles:

'The introduction of a European Prize for Literature shows that the European Union is more than politics and finance and sewage incinerators. It gives soul to the European Union. We are not just a conglomeration of financiers but an institution that has soul.'

She smiled at the camera until it was turned off and the screen went blank.

'Ah yes,' sighed Shimon Simonov, at his most fawning. 'How lucky you are. The European soul is healthy and strong. I thought I saw the great Russian soul walking along through the silver birches. It limped and walked with a stick. It was always ahead of me. Nearly out of sight. And then I lost it.'

Pyotr Stepanovich was staring at Shimon with a look which clearly said 'Wrap your fake Russian soul up and put it in your pocket. We are trying to get a grant here.'

No-one knows what Shimon Simonov would have gone on to say because at that moment one of the doors leading off the room slowly opened and Babikov's lodger, known only as The Serb, stepped into the room, smiling and reeking of wine fumes. He was tall and wore a pill-box hat and a green calf-length jacket with a theatrical appearance that had some insignia on it. With the unerring instinct of someone who recognises the most important person in the room, The Serb stepped forward and addressed himself to Madame Schultz:

'Holy Russia will rise again. In Schlisselburg,' he announced.

Madame Schultz was not sure that her Russian was up to the occasion. So she beamed.

Encouraged, The Serb took another step in her direction.

'But there are other forces. What about the other forces controlling us? The Shining Beings?' he enquired.

By this time Vasili Babikov had risen from his chair and was leading the Serb back to his quarters.

Nikolai put his head in his hands. Madame Schultz, however, sensing that the drama was over, continued with the conversation about soul.

'We think business can have soul too.' At this observation the room fell silent. 'Look at our lovely Manuel Barroso. President of the European Commission for many years. It was under his tenure that this European prize for literature was established to prove that we have soul. And he has gone straight to Goldman Sachs to continue his career and spread the word there.'

Nikolai put a restraining hand on the shoulder of Egor whose teeth were baring into a grimace.

As if things could not get worse, the afternoon sun chose at that precise moment to penetrate a crack in the green brocade cover of the parrot's cage and the parrot found his voice:

'Lenin's work will live on. The party is our helmsman. Communism will live forever!' shrieked the parrot.

Suddenly, Mrs Yelena Babikov wobbled to her feet, her lips and jowl trembling with emotion:

'And what are we supposed to do? He is our beloved family pet. Are we supposed to have him put down just because his ideas are a little old-fashioned? Well, I say no. We love and cherish him. Let him say whatever he thinks.'

'Bravo,' agreed Madame Schultz, who remembered her own anguish at having to leave her favourite pet cat behind in Brazil. In a flash she recognised that here was the true spirit of tolerance and compassion she was seeking: 'I shall let you know the result of your application by email as soon as I return.'

She restrained herself from announcing her verdict until she could announce the results to all the applicants simultaneously. In our bureaucracy lies our fairness, she reminded herself.

Nikolai had been appointed to escort her to Moskovski Station and spent much of the journey there enquiring about cisterns.

No sooner was Madame Shultz out of earshot than Egor Dudnik leapt to his feet, ran over to the wall and banged his head on it several times shouting:

'Bastards. They have ruined the 'Ode to Joy'. They play it as a formula on every tin-pot occasion. I hate them. They should all be shot. I've a good mind to go to Moscow and blow up everyone working for the European Union.'

'I hope you're not going to blow people up dressed like that,' said Pyotr Stepanovish, who had spotted that Egor still wore his pyjama top under his best summer shirt.

Shimon Simenov stood up:

'When I was drinking, I was a god. I could stride through Petersburg. I could knock people out. Now I'm creeping around saying "Excuse me" to European bureaucrats.'

The weary group said goodbye with no idea of the success or otherwise of their meeting.

Back in Moscow Madame Schultz found an email in her inbox. It was from Boeing Aircraft Manufacturers in Chicago. It seemed that the Serbian gentleman had managed to leave the Babikov household and crawl into a police station to report that his feet were missing. Having been admitted to a detoxification unit he had somehow ordered a Boeing 707 jet from America for his private use. Madame Schultz had received an email asking if the gentleman did have enough funds to purchase such an aircraft and whether the European Union was, indeed, standing guarantor. She clucked with impatience and deleted the email.

She then sent an email informing the Petersburg group that their application was successful and that as soon as they supplied the remaining 20% of the grant they would receive a cheque for 56,000 euros.

Madame Schultz surveyed her work with satisfaction. Was it possible that through her actions she had been instrumental in turning that great ship of state, Mother Russia, in a new direction that would avoid corruption and embrace moderation and tolerance? She hoped so. Having poured herself a drink, she settled down to watch a rather strange documentary about the conflict in the Ukraine and the righteousness of Russian actions there while puzzling briefly over the wailing sound that was coming from her guard's sentry box.

No-one had read the small print. The next morning telephones rang frantically between the members of the writers' group. The sum of 14,000 euros was impossible for them to raise between them. Finally, Nikolai telephoned his friend Fyodor and asked if there was any way the oligarch might help.

On the set of his fake documentary, Fyodor, dressed in his Night of the Wolf-Hook costume, approached the oligarch, who was seated in the producer's chair overlooking a location strewn with the ruins of blown-up tanks and the remnants of rocket grenades. He was a large, pear-shaped man with a fleshy but mobile face and a powerful lazy carnality. He wore black silk socks and an open-necked shirt.

'Good morning, Midas.' Fyodor sidled up to the oligarch. 'I thought I should tell you that I heard something that worried me a little. It concerns your campaign to run for president. There is a group of scally-wag intellectuals, writers and satirists who intend to bring out a magazine that refers to some unsavoury episodes in your past.'

A thunderclap of laughter erupted from the oligarch.

'How much will it cost to buy up all the copies?'

'I'm not sure.'

The oligarch wrote out a chit and handed it to Fyodor. 'Take this to the finance department. They will provide funds.'

The day after the cheque from the European Union arrived the Babikovs' apartment was unusually quiet. Having worked out the budget for printing and distributing the magazine, as well as a small fee for their creative endeavours, and, of course a substantial amount for the treatment of their friend, Ivan Persikov's cancer, the group had been left with two thousand euros each.

Vasili Babikov was at the tailor's ordering several new suits. Egor Dudnik was investigating the price of changing his name by deed poll. Shimon Simonov was browsing in his favourite bookshop and Nikolai Pestov was consulting plumbers, regretting only that the money was still not enough to buy the Korsakovs out. Pyotr Stepanovich was dealing with a crisis at the Dostoyevsky Museum. One of the tenants of an apartment in the building had been indulging in some sadomasochistic practices with a young prostitute. Unfortunately, he had left the apartment and forgotten about her. She was bound on his bed with various straps of leather paraphernalia and gagged with gaffer tape. Having managed to free herself, she was hopping from flat to flat pressing the doorbells with her nose in order to get help. Eventually she had burst into the Dostoyevsky Museum, interrupting an American professor of Russian Literature and his fourteen students. The American was demanding his money back while Pyotr tried to explain that Dostoyevsky himself might have appreciated such a scene. Pyotr finally gave in and reimbursed the professor and his fourteen students.

'At least we've got rid of the death penalty,' he shouted after the departing Americans as he tried to disentangle the prostitute from her harness.

The next day another surprise awaited the writers' group. Vasili Babikov summoned them to his apartment, where he sat at the table with multiple rolls of roubles piled in front of him. He poured a glass of vodka for each of them.

'Friends,' he announced when they were all seated. 'We have received a commission and a massive increase in our funds. Fyodor's oligarch is apparently determined to spend a short amount of time in prison to boost his credentials as a dissident and as a genuine opponent to the current government in his campaign for the presidency. Apparently, our Midas caught sight of a newspaper photograph of one of the Pussy Riot girls in jail. She was looking demure at a desk in her cell and writing her prison letters, corresponding with some Slovenian radical with an unpronounceable name. Their correspondence contained references to Hegel and Demosthenes. The oligarch was impressed. He has commissioned us to write his prison letters. The letters must be packed with similar intellectual and cultural references. He has paid us handsomely in advance. I'm sure we can conjure up something, gentlemen. After all, it was we Russians who gave the world the word "intelligentzia"!'

The group stared in astonishment at the bundles of roubles on the table. Then Egor enquired tentatively, 'And what are we to do about our creative attempts to advance the cause of moderation in our anti-corruption magazine for the European Union?'

Vasili leaned back precariously in his chair. 'I think you will find that Midas the oligarch has already bought up all the copies.'

Egor frowned. 'But we haven't written it yet.'

'Exactly. We will explain to the E.U. at some future date that it sold like hot cakes. History has taught us always to remember that pretending is better than believing. In fact, we should drink to the E.U. and its benefits, especially on behalf of Ivan Persikov who is, at this minute, receiving treatment for his cancer, courtesy of the E.U. grant.'

The group rose merrily to their feet to make a toast. Vasili smiled and raised his glass but before he could say any more Egor scrambled onto his chair and shouted with glee:

'Death to moderation.' He tossed back his vodka and hurled the empty glass over his shoulder. Everyone in turn followed his example, clambering on their chairs, drinking and flinging their tumblers over their shoulders until they were surrounded by a lake of shattered glass.

Vasili gestured for them to sit down again.

'Meanwhile, the prison letters must be our priority. There is a demonstration next month and the oligarch is planning to be arrested while attending it. We need to get a move on.'

*

Later that afternoon, Nikolai Timurovich Pestov sat at the table in his apartment opposite Mr and Mrs Korsakov. The piles of roubles upon which their eyes were fixed were clearly enough to buy them out. He cleared his throat and spoke:

'Mr and Mrs Korsakov. I have a proposition to make.'

FABLE OF A MISSING WORD

The celebration in the Amerindian village of Pakuri was to be held that afternoon. Uncle Horace, speech-maker in chief, stepped out onto the top step of his house and surveyed the scene. It was early morning. Wooden houses thatched with dalibana leaf stood silently on their stilts in the white sand. Uncle Horace had already bathed in the creek at the back of the house, splashing himself with the creek water that vegetation had stained a dark red, the colour of Pepsi-Cola. Now he stood outside his house, the notes for the speech in his hand, hoping to attract attention. Putting on his glasses, he held the notes at arm's length and made a conspicuous study of them. Uncle Horace was proud to be the most proficient Lokono Arawak speaker in the village. Arawak, a language that harked back to the days before Columbus, was still spoken, although mainly by the elders. But at that hour in the morning there was no-one present to witness his preparations. There was only the sound of the keskidee birds in the trees and the occasional yellow flash as one flew by. Disappointed at the lack of an audience he folded the notes for his speech and replaced them in his top pocket. Then he turned round and went back inside.

72

On the other side of the village Lucas Peters swung his legs out of the hammock, jumped to the floor and upturned the hammock to shake out some cassava crumbs. The family party was to celebrate his achievements. He had been to England and returned with a degree in Rainforest Archaeology. His mother's house where he had been born stood near the edge of the village in the area where the sand came to an end and the grasses, muri bushes and awara trees began. Her house was elevated a foot or so from the ground on uneven stilts. It consisted of one room not more than twelve foot square. The grey wooden plank walls remained unpainted. The bed where his mother slept occupied most of the space. There was barely enough room for his hammock but he only expected to be there for a few days.

At the age of eighty-one his mother could still manage to make cassava bread and weave hammocks. On Sundays, without fail, she swept out the church. At night when he lay there he tried to hear the words she was saying as she whispered her prayers but they were always inaudible. Lucas was concerned about her. Every now and then her heart jumped and fluttered like a small patwa fish and made her stand still until the heart found its regular beat again. Planting and weeding the cassava farm had become more of an effort.

When his mother went to bathe, Lucas dressed, pulled on his blue jeans and his heavy bush boots. His black hair had grown long enough to touch the collar of his yellow shirt. He left the house and stood outside next to where the sifter hung on the wall. A white enamel bucket and stack of white plates on a bench dazzled his eyes in the bright morning sun.

At the age of forty-five Lucas had finally managed to secure enough funds to study at the University of London. During his period away in England he had tried to work out how he could apply his newly acquired knowledge of ancient indigenous farming techniques in a way that would help his own people. Even as a child he had worried about the condition of his Arawak village and fretted over how to make things better. He would lie in his hammock and plan the defence of the village against intruders. Now he wanted to experiment with the idea of reviving the raised field farming techniques that had been used centuries ago. He had ideas too of using solar-powered computers to link Amerindian communities across the country. The important thing is, he thought, to be inventive. Old traditions could be revived, renewed and modernised if only people would use their intelligence and imagination.

The week after he returned from England the radio station in Georgetown recorded an interview with him about his degree. The next day, just as the programme was being broadcast, Lucas was in town walking past a house in Camp Street where the radio was on. He could hear a young black girl saying in amazement to her mother:

'Hear the man on the radio, Mummy. You hear how buck man could talk?'

'They still think we are stupid,' he told his brother when he returned to the village and reported what he had heard.

Now he watched as his mother made her way back to the house. There was a lightness and spring in her step. She was wearing her best green cotton dress, and checked her white hair with her hand as she walked, to ensure that it was neatly plaited. Mai, as they called her, preferred to walk barefoot even when the sand beneath her feet was burning hot. If there was one place his mother hated it was Georgetown. Whenever she was obliged to go there, she returned home as quickly as possible and headed for the bush. At home she spoke Arawak. The youngsters now spoke mainly in English. They understood Arawak but rarely spoke it. But Mai liked to use her own language.

It had been Mai's idea to celebrate her son's achievement. What this degree business was all about she was not too sure but he had been away for a long time and mixed with a lot of white people to get it. She decided a small party was in order.

'Just a quiet celebration with the family. Uncle Horace can make a speech.'

By the time afternoon came, Uncle Horace had fixed everything up beneath the coconut trees which shaded his house. A small table, leaning slightly to one side, perched on the sand in front of the house. On it he had laid a white cloth and set out two bottles of vodka with some glasses, jugs of coconut water and a pink hibiscus blossom in a jam jar.

Lucas was related to half the people in the village. The family started to gather. His two oldest uncles came and shook him earnestly by the hand, almost shyly, not saying anything but nodding their heads with toothless grins. Uncles, aunts, cousins and their children milled around. Auntie Zizi huffed and puffed her way over to Uncle Horace's house brandishing two bottles of rum.

'Congrats Lucas. Is wha yuh want? Fast and Nasty or Cheap and Sweet? Help yourself.'

She put the rum on the table and started pouring out glasses of coconut water for the children.

It was a scorching hot afternoon. Uncle Horace kept himself a little apart from the crowd in order to emphasise the solemnity of his speech-making duties. Gradually, people began to assemble, sitting down on logs, squatting in the sand, brushing grit off the sun-faded wooden benches and making themselves comfortable. Uncle Horace poured himself a vodka and took up his place behind the table. He cleared his throat and waited for everyone to settle down.

Always on these occasions, Uncle Horace spoke Lokono Arawak. He considered himself to be the master and commander of the language. Younger members of the community consulted him should they ever want to know an Arawak word – which they rarely did. He seldom failed them. When people came to listen to Uncle Horace, the voices of ancestors who had lived there for thousands of years before the arrival of Columbus could be heard again and Uncle Horace was proud to be a conduit to the past in that way.

He coughed and glared at Auntie Zizi who was still talking loudly. Finally everyone became silent and the only sounds came from a keskidee in the bush and a dog barking somewhere on the other side of the village. The sun blazed down. Uncle Horace swallowed some vodka and began his formal speech:

'Halekwa ha, tu kasakabu . . .'

Lucas's brother Mart, wearing his black felt hat, dark glasses and a pendant round his neck came and crouched down beside Lucas. He lifted up his glasses and winked at his brother. They had sat through many of these speeches together.

Now although Uncle Horace made his speech almost entirely in Lokono Arawak, he had been obliged to use some English words. 'London University,' 'aeroplane' and 'Queen of England' came up frequently. His voice was thin and wavery so that people had to lean forward to hear him. After every other sentence he helped himself to more vodka. Soon he began to list to one side. His pauses became more and more frequent.

Into one of these pauses, striding across the sand, burst Uncle Tommy. Uncle Tommy was raw Arawak. His mouth was twisted over an upper tooth that protruded from the side of his mouth. He was late because he had just returned from his farm five miles upriver where he had been weeding all day and had not had time to smarten up for the party. He had paddled his canoe as hard as he could to be back in time and now he pushed his way amongst the group to make room for himself on one of the logs. He was barefoot, smelling of sweat and wearing a torn grey vest, with his trouser legs rolled up to the calves of his muscular brown legs. On his head he wore a black and white baseball cap. He listened carefully as Uncle Horace spoke. It was the climax of the speech and Lucas and the Queen of England were making several appearances together.

When Uncle Horace brought his speech to its conclusion there was a round of applause. He folded his notes and was putting them in his shirt pocket, about to sit down, when Uncle Tommy stood up, made his way to the table and, holding on to the edges of it with his gnarled hands, faced the crowd and began to speak. He spoke pure and unhesitating Arawak from the heart:

'I want to speak because I remember Lucas from when he was a baby. We called him Horotoshi because he had no hair. Calabash-head we called him, or sometimes we called him Potakashi because he looked like an old, bald-headed Portuguese man. His brother we called Korihi because he scampered everywhere like a rat. His mother we called Kaimahu because she was often vexed with them. And now look what Calabash-head has done. He has gone away and studied in some far off place with white people. He has even learned to speak like

77

them. That Calabash-head is now full of learning. I can't read or write, but he can. Let us all drink to Calabash-head. Pass me some bambeli.'

People cheered and passed Uncle Tommy a bowl of bambeli. He raised the bowl to his lips, drank it down and turned to spit out the dregs behind him. Lucas's brother Mart started to tease Uncle Horace:

'Uncle Horace, I thought you supposed to be the chief Arawak speaker. Yuh hear Uncle Tommy? He din use no English words. An he drinkin pure bambeli like an Arawak man, not vodka.'

Uncle Horace's face turned an even darker shade of bronze.

'I have to use some English words. The youngsters don't speak enough Arawak. I have to say some things in English,' he protested.

Clearly upset, he threw his plastic cup down in the sand, then took out his speech from his pocket, scrunched it up and threw it after the cup. Turning his head away from people who were staring at him, he stomped off and stood by himself on the edge of the village where the sand ended and the tall grasses began. The sun was beginning to set. Shadows from the coconut tree leaves lay in jagged slashes on the ground in front of him.

People started to say goodbye and drift away. Mart put his hand on his brother's shoulder:

'Look at Uncle Horace,' he said. 'We better do something.'

They looked over at where Uncle Horace stood miserably beneath the trees, staring at his feet.

Lucas stood up. He and Mart fetched Uncle Tommy and the three of them trudged through the sand to where Uncle Horace stood beneath the trees. Lucas faced Uncle Horace.

'Ok. We'll settle this business about who is the chief Arawak speaker before the sun goes down. I'm going to ask you both a question. He took each uncle by the arm and stood them facing each other as if for a duel. Sensing that some sort of challenge was taking place and curious to see what was happening, a few people returned and stood in a semi-circle around the two men.

Lucas shut his eyes and bit his lip in concentration:

'Right. Ok. I've got it. Which one of you can tell me the Arawak word for . . . padlock?'

There was a deadly hush under the trees. Both men stared at each other as they racked their brains. Overhead a huge army of clouds was marching across the sky from Venezuela. A long silence ensued. Spots of rain fell. Uncle Tommy's mouth twisted up more than ever. His eyes shifted back and forth between the sky and the ground. Uncle Horace stood there stroking his chin. Then Uncle Tommy spoke up:

'We don' have such a word. The Arawak language existed before white people brought iron. So the word doesn't exist in Arawak,' he announced, pleased to have found a way of solving the problem.

Uncle Horace saw his opportunity and pounced.

'Ah, but you have to be wily. You have to think around this problem. You must ask yourself what is it that a padlock does. A padlock holds on to something tight. A padlock will never let go. It will grip to the death. And what else grips to the death? What is it that has massively powerful front legs with unretractable claws? IT'S AN ANTEATER.'

Uncle Horace's chest swelled with triumph:

'So the Arawak for a padlock would be – Baremo Okotu. The Grasp of the Anteater.'

79

Spontaneous cheers and applause rose from a few people who had come to see what was happening. Uncle Tommy threw his cap in the air and ceded defeat. Lucas announced:

'I pronounce Uncle Horace chief Arawak speaker of the village.'

Uncle Horace bowed and shook Uncle Tommy by the hand. Then he said goodnight and strode proudly back to his house as if he were walking through the sky.

The next morning Lucas walked over to his brother's house. Mart was outside the house starting work on his carving. He was contemplating the huge block of wood in front of him:

'Wha yuh makin there?'

'I think I've found a giant anteater in this block of wood.' Mart grinned as he wielded his chisel. 'I goin let him out.'

THE DREAM OF OCALAN
A Fable

That part of the Syrian desert is a plateau of basement rock covered by layers of horizontally bedded sediment forming massive sand plains and dunes. Wind is the sculptor. It shapes the orange dunes into sandy hillocks and chisels out sharp-edged basins lined with dark shadows only to re-arrange everything the next day into an altered landscape of ridges and sand-seas. Nothing is permanent.

Walking across those dunes through shifting sands, a figure rippled in the light. In the distance behind him was a huge blackened ruin of a tower. A hot wind blew in his face. He stopped to shake some of the gritty sand from his shirt sleeves and look back. The burnt-out edge of the tower was ratcheted like the edge of a film strip, black with tiny transparent rectangles where the light came through. Even now he felt as if he were still running to escape from that oven, the soles of his feet parched.

He trudged on through the heat. The land flattened out into a dusty rock-strewn wilderness with patches of grass. This was Rojava. He was heading for the town of Qamishli to look for his friend Ardil. There were unfinished conversations between them that had started many years earlier. What had become of Ardil? He was curious to know.

As he came closer to the town something on the ground caught his eye. A white asphodel plant poked out from the shelter of a few rocks. Amazed that a plant could survive in such surroundings he bent to look at it. A clump of delicate white flowers branched out from silvery-grey spiky foliage. Each flower had six starry white petals. On impulse he stooped to pick it. The thick-stemmed plant resisted his efforts with surprising tenacity. He remembered learning at school about the asphodel meadows – an area of the underworld reserved for the souls of ordinary people who had done nothing special in their lives, nothing particularly good or bad. He twisted and tugged. It would not come away. Finally, regretting that he had bent the stem, he gave up and left the flower drooping.

On the outskirts of the city he made his way through dried mud streets and squat houses made of clay with straw roofs. Dogs barked as he walked along. Towards the centre of town the clay hovels were replaced by cinderblock and brick houses and then by tall white blocks of flats with balconies in well-laid out dusty streets. He stopped and studied a sign that said Qamislo. So the name had been changed from Qamishli to the Kurdish version. What does that mean? he wondered.

He found Ardil in a meeting. The meeting was taking place in a large, high-ceilinged room above a bakery. He slipped in and stood at the back. The smell of flat breads baking drifted up from below mingled with the aroma of his favourite pastries filled with feta cheese. Through open windows could be heard the harsh shouts of market traders in the street outside. Forty or so men and women were seated, crammed together on what looked like school benches arranged in circles.

Ardil was immediately recognisable even after all those years. He was wearing a black t-shirt and jeans and still had his beloved camera slung round his neck. He looked older and more confident. His eyes held that familiar humorous glint and his moustache bristled with energy as he leaned forward to emphasise the points he was making. He brandished a hand-made booklet to which he referred, sometimes reading passages from it to illustrate what he was saying or to look for guidance. It seemed that the French owners of one of the local cement factories had disappeared as a result of the war and there was a debate about how to occupy, requisition and manage the factory. At that moment a fierce argument broke out in the room. A stout woman with an ocean of wavy brown hair stood up to complain that her husband would not have enough time to be involved because he had to run their leather shop and take the children to school. The matter was resolved amidst laughter and she sat down again.

No-one took any notice of the traveller who had appeared from the desert and who was leaning against the back wall. As he listened, he recognised that Ardil was now putting into practice some of the ideas that they had discussed many years before. In those days he used to argue with Ardil all night in cafes, drinking tea, smoking endless cigarettes and still talking as they made their way to university in the morning. He had considered himself the pragmatist. Ardil, he thought, was too idealistic. Ardil had stayed behind in Syria with his Kurdish community whereas he had escaped and gone to England to study computer engineering with the hope of ending up one day in Silicon Valley.

In the meeting room people were smiling. The community seemed to have been transformed since he was last there although he had only visited a few times before when he stayed with Ardil's family. Now the energised townsfolk were doing things differently. There was talk of collectivising land, occupying abandoned workplaces, re-populating empty villages. The discussions took place in a carefree atmosphere, as if it were the easiest and most sensible thing in the world to achieve such things even in the middle of a war zone and surrounded by destruction. He twisted his head round until he could read the title printed on the front of Ardil's booklet. It said: *The Dream of Ocalan* and in smaller letters underneath *Notes from the Sea of Marmara*. Some people were fanning themselves with their copies.

The meeting was breaking up. A team had been appointed to organise the cement factory. Another group had been formed to deal with some problems involving the disposal of street garbage. Just then a short man wearing his military cap and fatigues arrived and with a sense of urgency pushed his way through the group to show Ardil something on his mobile phone. Ardil jumped to his feet with an expression of dismay. People gathered around. The atmosphere changed. After a brief discussion it was decided that everyone must report to their local militia group. The U.S. troops were withdrawing as they spoke. There were already reports of Turkish troops gathering on the border. Ardil grabbed his leather shoulder bag and headed for the door. For a moment he glanced up towards the back of the room but either he did not see or did not recognise his old acquaintance.

He watched Ardil disappear. The room emptied. He went over to one of the benches and picked up a discarded booklet.

It was written in Kurdish and English. He stuffed it in his pocket. Clearly it would be impossible to find Ardil again in these circumstances. But somehow his curiosity had been satisfied. He decided to return home. For a moment he stood in the doorway and felt confused as to where his real home lay.

He headed back out of town retracing the way he had come, clutching his sandals in his hand. They had been chafing his feet and he preferred to travel barefoot. On the outskirts of town he rested for a while on the stone trough where animals came to drink. There he examined his blisters and decided to risk putting his sandals on again. Two military Toyota vehicles sped past him on their way out of the city. He continued on his journey, thinking about what he had just seen: the defiant woman arguing her case; the atmosphere of camaraderie amongst ordinary people; the decision to occupy the factory. All these things he considered as he walked. After a mile or so he came once more upon the small pile of rocks that held the asphodel plant. It was still there, its starry blooms upright again, no longer drooping. He paused. The vitality and resilience of the flower attracted him. He plucked one small blossom from the spray and folded it between the leaves of the booklet before putting it back in his pocket.

It was getting late. A great crimson balloon-sun rested lightly above the horizon, burning through the dust. He looked ahead seeking the tower in order to find his bearings. The place where he thought the tower had once been was now enveloped in a black cloud. All the same he headed in that direction occasionally feeling in his pocket for the booklet. *The Dream of Ocalan. Notes from the Sea of Marmara.* The name itself sounded like the murmur of waves in the dryness of the desert.

85

Soothing and refreshing. He had read some of it as he walked. Reading it exhilarated him. It was a political tract but in straightforward language and it opened out the top of his head into a galaxy of new ideas blown there by a solar wind. He wished he could take Ardil by the arm and that they could go for a drink of handmade wine in one of the Tel Tamer bars they had secretly frequented as students and where they could continue their long conversations. He would tell Ardil that he understood better what he was trying to do and that he admired him for it.

He looked up from the booklet. A huge wide pillar of black dust the size of half a city was making its way towards him. Even at a distance the sand and grit were beginning to whip up and sting his face. To his left was an outcrop of grey rocks. He recognised it as one of the stable landmarks from which the few nomads in the region took their bearings. Earlier he had seen one of them, standing some distance away, alone in the desert with his goat. The man had waved at him. There was nothing he could do but try to shelter beneath the spur of rocks. He pulled his cotton scarf over his head and held it up to protect his eyes and mouth but soon he was choking on a whirlwind of dust, sightless and sand-blind. Tank after tank roared past. Minutes later he heard the whine of F16 bombers overhead. He felt a sudden chill of fear for the citizens of Qamislo.

When everything grew quiet again he pushed on. And who knows whether it took a short time or a long time but eventually the tower towards which he had been heading rose up in front of him, a tall blackened honeycomb of charred flats. An image came back to him, a memory of black smoke that contained a spiky dancing thistle of crimson flame. And a memory of falling. A long fall. It should have been more of a surprise to him than it was to find himself back in London, in West London at one end of Lancaster Road, to be precise. It had been a long walk. Now the harsh metallic energy of the city assaulted him. The blaring noise of traffic hurt his ears. People were shouting. There seemed to be some sort of demonstration around him in the street. Hardly able to keep up as they marched was a severely disabled man with a twisted jerky gait. He walked on the balls of his feet, leaning backwards at an angle and encouraging the protesters as they slowly made their way forward.

The traveller decided to keep moving. In an attempt to avoid the confusion he stepped down into the gutter and edged his way past the crowd. He made his way to a small park which contained a children's playground. The playground was closed for the evening and all was quiet. He jumped over the railings and climbed up the ladder of the children's slide to where he could get a better view from the tiny landing at the top. Below, on the other side of the railings, the disabled man was bending down to pick up something from the pavement. It was his copy of *The Dream of Ocalan* which must have fallen from his pocket. He put his hand there to check. Yes. The booklet had gone. He watched the man flick through the pages and then become absorbed in the content, letting the dried asphodel flower float zig-zagging to the pavement. And then it seemed as though the whole playground below him was a meadow of asphodel plants. The silvery-grey plants with white starry flowers had spread not only over the playground but over some of the adjacent street as well. And standing there not fifty yards away was Ardil, up to his knees in the meadow flowers. Puzzled, he patted himself down to see if his clothes and the cotton scarf around his neck were still full of desert sand from the journey. It was then that he realised that he himself was made of nothing more than rubble and grit and wind.

ANNA KARENINA AND MADAME BOVARY DISCUSS THEIR SUICIDES

Of the many invisible cities described by Calvino there is one remarkable city that is missing. If you approach this city by road you can see the main station on the outskirts. A handful of people loiter on the platform. It is only when you enter the missing city that you understand it consists of nothing but waiting spaces: private waiting rooms, public waiting rooms, foyers, lobbies, ante-rooms, precincts set aside for queuing, courtyards designed for hanging about. The entire city is constructed for the sole purpose of waiting.

The waiting rooms are of different historical periods and serve different purposes. Some are rooms where ambassadors and dignitaries wait before being called in to be presented to the emperor or caliph or president. These high-ceilinged rooms have wallcoverings, usually crimson and mainly of silk, as well as elaborately embossed carpets. Liveried servants wait to usher in the chosen elite into the hallowed presence but, of course, that moment never arrives. Then there are dentists' and doctors' waiting rooms where patients flick through magazines and no-one is ever called in to see the consultant. Other groups assemble in the dank, badly lit waiting rooms of railway stations with old benches and dated posters where, naturally, no train puts in an appearance. People mingle in theatre foyers for drinks before a show which they will never see. Students gather together and talk a little as they wait outside the examination room. Through the window they can see the invigilator laying out exam papers meticulously, one on each desk, for an exam they will never sit. And, of course, two actors, costumed as tramps, wait endlessly in the wings ready to step onto a brightly lit stage whose set is nothing more than a country road and one tree.

Rooms on different floors are linked by moving escalators where people wait to progress from one level to another, slowly rising or descending until they can resume waiting elsewhere. From a distance the city appears to be full of people moving around meaningfully occupied, but this is not the case.

Some people believe that the city is really an enormous art installation where people wander from one period of history and from one experience to another but in reality, the experience is always the same, the experience of waiting. All the same, there are no signs of serious discontent in the population. Hope keeps people quiescent. Expectancy is all.

The meeting between the two women took place in a spacious room on the second floor of a large four-storey house. They were seated, engrossed in conversation, on a high-backed oak settle which also served as a storage chest. Anna Karenina was in a light-hearted frame of mind. Over her blue dress she wore a pale cashmere shawl embroidered with thin wool in a floral pattern round the edges. Her face was animated, her grey eyes alight with surprise and curiosity as she turned to Emma Bovary.

'Do you mean that your husband never suspected anything?'

Emma Bovary was the shorter of the two with a sturdy body suggesting peasant stock. Her shiny black hair was styled a la Chinoise, parted in the middle with a neat knot on top. She wore a cream cotton dress that fitted tightly over her plump breasts, and smart black boots that showed off her ankles to advantage. Mistaking Anna's curiosity for admiration, Emma cocked her head to one side and gave a small smile of satisfaction.

'Charles never had any idea. Not a clue.'

Anna managed to suppress a hint of disapproval. 'How did you manage that?'

'Well, in some ways I always thought Charles was an imbecile. He had absolutely no ambition. I would have liked our name to be famous. He was just content to bumble about as a country doctor. I was furious once when he botched an operation that could have made our names. Anyway, my beloved Charles never noticed a thing. I even used to slip out of bed early in the mornings to meet my lover, Rodolphe, in the arbour at the end of the garden and Charles never knew.' Emma giggled. 'Oh yes. And he never knew about Leon either. Heaven knows why he didn't spot what was going on. Didn't your husband ever suspect anything?'

Anna raised a disdainful eyebrow as she recalled the early days of her affair with Vronsky and her husband's reaction.

'Oh Karenin – he sniffed something from the first moment. He didn't exactly suspect anything himself but he noticed that people were talking about me and Vronsky and he didn't like that. It was all a matter of appearances for him. I think he just refused to believe it was possible that I should do such a thing. But anyway, in the end I told him.'

Emma looked appalled. 'You told him?'

Anna nodded and smiled. 'I really don't like living with that sort of deceit. And Vronsky hated being involved in lies. He was too honourable. He couldn't have tolerated it for long.'

Emma looked directly at Anna and the freshness, openness and self-possession she saw in that lovely face made her feel inferior and a little cheap. Perhaps Anna was not capable of being sly or duplicitous? And what was all this about honour? If confessing the truth to one's husband was the price of honour, she could do without it. But perhaps this was how the aristocracy always behaved, Emma wondered. How odd. She had been thrilled to find that her new friend was a member of the Russian nobility and listened enthralled as Anna talked about Prince This and Princess That and casually referred to footmen and servants. 'Oh, was your Vronsky a count?' Emma had exclaimed, her eyes widening in awe. And Anna had shrugged and laughed as if it were nothing.

Feeling that she had not been completely straightforward about her confession to Karenin, Anna hastened to explain: 'Well actually, I was pregnant with Vronsky's child. I had to tell him.'

'Oh how awful. Thank heavens that never happened to me. One child was bad enough.' Emma lowered her voice to a whisper. 'Did you find that once you had fallen for someone else you suddenly couldn't stand your child? I remember shoving my daughter away and thinking she was an ugly little so and so. But then, I was obsessed with Rodolphe.'

Anna was a little taken aback.

'Oh no. I still loved my son with Karenin . . . at least I think I did. In fact I once risked everything to visit him secretly on his birthday. But I know what you mean. When things were going well with Vronsky I never gave my son a second thought. And I do remember coming home at one point after I'd been with Vronsky and thinking what a disappointment my son was. He just seemed so tedious and unexceptional. Vronsky occupied my thoughts entirely.'

Emma nodded in sympathy.

'Children get in the way, don't they? When Rodolphe and I were planning to run away together he asked what we should do about my daughter. Without thinking I just said, "We'll take her with us".' Emma shook her head in exasperation. 'That was my big mistake. It must have put him off. I should have said I'd leave her behind.' Emma straightened the long skirts of her dress and pushed her lips out in a defiant pout. 'Anyway, my husband ate slowly. That's enough to drive anyone mad.'

'Oh, my husband was maddeningly stubborn and aloof. You can't imagine.' A shadow crossed Anna's face and she twisted her hands together as she blurted out, 'To be honest, when my daughter was born, Vronsky's child, that is, I just didn't take to her. I felt bad about it but I never really liked her. Not even when she was ill. I think I was scared because I knew Vronsky had always disliked family life and here I was trapping him into domesticity. Worse still, according to Russian law I was still married to Karenin and so the child had to take the name Karenin unless my husband agreed to give me a divorce so that I could re-marry. The name business disturbed Vronsky no end. Besides, after the birth I nearly died. Vronsky was so distraught he tried to shoot himself.'

Emma was impressed and a little envious. No-one had ever tried to kill themselves on her behalf. She searched for a comparable experience of her own.

'I was desperately ill too. I nearly died when Rodolphe sent me a letter saying the elopement was off and he was leaving. In fact I was just going to throw myself out of the window when Charles happened to call me down to supper. It would have been better if I'd done away with myself then. Better that way than arsenic, I can tell you. Anyway, I had a nervous collapse that lasted for months.'

The two women lapsed into silence, each of them caught up in her own thoughts.

After a few minutes, Emma got up and walked across the wooden floor to the window on her side of the room. Calico curtains hung there. The canary-coloured wallpaper around the window was peeling with damp. She leaned her elbows on the window sill and looked out over the market square of Yonville l'Abbaye. Nothing had changed. The plaster figure of a Cupid with his finger on his lips still stood on the gate of the notary's house opposite. In the distance she could see the flat and characterless landscape typical of that region of France. Before long she was overcome with the familiar feeling of suffocation. She was stifled with ennui. 'Oh why, dear God, did I marry him?' she repeated again and again. Down in the depth of her soul Emma Bovary was waiting and longing for something to happen. That was the enduring image of her existence. The summary of her life. Waiting and longing. After a while she broke away and returned to her conversation with Anna:

'Was it love at first sight for you?' Emma enquired, inspecting the heel of her boot as she settled back down beside her companion. 'I always thought love should strike like a clap of thunder.'

Anna Karenina gave the matter careful consideration.

'Well no, not really. I met Vronsky in a railway station. Nothing happened at the time although I could sense I had made an impression on him. There'd been an accident. A guard died. Vronsky very generously offered money to the man's family. I knew immediately that he'd done it to impress me. I saw him later in the house . . . there was something. But nothing really happened until the ball that was being held for Kitty, my young sister-in-law. I shouldn't have behaved as I did.' Anna turned to Emma and made a slight grimace of remorse. 'Vronsky was more or less betrothed to Kitty. But what happened between me and Vronsky that night was irresistible. It was overpowering. We were both incapable of withstanding it.' Anna rolled her eyes and threw her head back and for a moment Emma looked at her and saw in her eager face something strange and diabolical and enchanting. 'But when I was leaving Moscow the next day to catch the train home to Petersburg I remember thinking, "Thank goodness that bit of excitement is over and from now on my life, my nice everyday life, will go on as before." But halfway home when I got off the train for some fresh air, Vronsky was there on the platform. He'd followed me.' Anna's eyes shone as she leaned against the high back of the settle.

Not to be outdone, Emma chattered on.

'I went to a ball once. We were invited to the home of the Marquis de Andervilliers. Charles had cured his abscess. That one contact with the rich changed me forever. I saw that my provincial life was dull, dull, dull. I longed to go to Paris and mix with . . . well . . . a better class of person. The day after the ball I bought myself a street map of Paris so that I could imagine shopping there.'

But Anna Karenina was not listening. At that moment, she left the seat, frowning, and hurried towards the window on her side of the room. The tall leaded window was set in wooden panelling. It overlooked a Moscow courtyard which had its gates already wide open to receive a carriage. Anna glanced out of the window and then began pacing up and down. Why did Vronsky always have to stay out so late? He was growing cold towards her, no doubt about it. He must know how miserable she was in Moscow. And there was still no news from Karenin about a divorce. She thought she heard the sound of carriage wheels on the cobbles and hurried back to the window. No. No sign of him. This is not living, she thought. Endlessly waiting for a solution that never comes is not living. I know he's getting tired of me. Why doesn't he come? It doesn't even matter if he doesn't love me. As long as he's here. The strain and anxiety of her situation caused a change in Anna's characteristically cheerful temperament. She bit her lip, shook her head and returned slowly to where she had been sitting.

Emma could not help noticing how graceful Anna was when she walked.

'How do you keep that lovely figure? I had to drink vinegar to keep slim.'

Anna ignored the question and posed one of her own as she sat down: 'What happened anyway with your Rodolphe and your Leon?' There was something sharp, almost dismissive, in the tone of her voice.

Emma sighed. 'Well Rodolphe was rich. He owned a chateau nearby. He was really attracted to me. We went riding together. Charles encouraged it – he thought it was good for my health. We started an affair. I became really bold. I couldn't stop myself. One morning when Charles was at work I ran all the way over to the chateau and burst in on him.' Emma held her hand to her mouth and her eyes flashed with amusement as she recalled her own behaviour. 'It was lust,' she admitted. 'I couldn't keep away from him.'

Anna found Emma Bovary entertaining and a welcome distraction from her own thoughts. She could see how men would be attracted to this pert creature with her red lips and wayward manner.

Emma rattled on: 'After that I went to the chateau whenever I could although Rodolphe warned me that I was becoming reckless. Now I realise I gave him too many gifts, expensive riding-whips, cigar cases, that sort of thing. I became over-sentimental too, talking to him in baby language which got on his nerves. And I was borrowing money like there was no tomorrow, ordering clothes and travelling bags for myself, thinking we were going away together. Then, out of the blue, he did a bunk. How despicable is that?'

Emma let out a hiss of disgust. She took some eau de cologne from a small bottle and sprinkled it on her arms.

'Go on.' At that moment Anna chose to be a listener, fearful of what she might reveal about herself if she talked.

Feeling flattered, Emma continued: 'Well then, Leon was somebody else I'd taken a fancy to. You've no idea how boring life is in the provinces. But Leon moved away to Rouen before anything happened. Then after the disaster with Rodolphe, I bumped into Leon again. He was sweet. We had this amazing ride in a horse-drawn cab. We just pulled the curtains and got on with it. I'd been worried that he'd be too timid. But he wasn't. I don't know why but after that I became more careless, sort of slapdash. I didn't really bother about anything anymore.

I paid everything on credit. Signed promissory notes. Spent a lot on clothes. I forged bills for the piano classes I pretended to Charles I was having – my excuse for going to Rouen. I was getting into huge debt. Trying to dodge bailiffs. Now I can see that everything was going to pieces.'

'Were you jealous?' asked Anna.

Emma held her hands in front of her to study the nails she had shaped so carefully. She thought for a moment and then replied: 'Not really. But I was pushy. I see that now. I demanded Leon wrote me love poems. I kept turning up at his office and he didn't like it. I'd made the same mistake with Rodolphe. Were you jealous of Vronsky?'

Anna stared straight ahead with a brooding look in her grey eyes.

'I was jealous of everything. Jealous of every minute I was not with him. I was even jealous of my child's nurse. I wanted total possession. "Love for man is a thing apart. 'Tis woman's whole existence." Have you read any Byron?'

Emma shook her head. 'I used to read Walter Scott at the convent. And I loved all those romances and the stories about martyred women. Passion. That's what I wanted.'

Anna gave a wry smile.

'I wrote a little myself. Children's stories, mainly. And I once re-wrote the first sentence of that famous novel by Jane Austen. She was all the rage with us at the time. My version went: "It is a truth not universally acknowledged that all married women, even when they are perfectly contented, are still looking for a husband." It's a sentence almost as famous as the one at the beginning of my own life story.' She pointed to the Penguin Classic copy of Tolstoy's *Anna Karenin* that lay beside her on the bench.

Emma gave a puzzled shrug and pulled her own Penguin Classic copy of *Madame Bovary* out of a drawstring bag. She frowned at the cover.

'I don't know why they've put me in that weird outfit. They should have used my ball dress. Pale saffron yellow with three bouquets of pompom roses trimmed with green. Satin slippers too.' She flicked through the pages of her life story. 'Oh, I'm such a fool. I hadn't realised that Leon held such a candle for me for all that time. I should have guessed and done something about it before he left.'

She came to the part of the book which described her long, drawn-out death. Her lips puckered with distaste.

'Why did he have to say my tongue was protruding like that? And black liquid was coming out of my mouth? Sometimes I wonder if Flaubert even liked me.'

Anna felt a surge of affection for her. 'Why did you do it?'

'Kill myself?' Emma took a deep breath. 'Debt. It was poverty that did me in, not adultery. I was desperate. Always fleeing debt collectors. Running from bailiffs. I just rushed into the pharmacy, grabbed a handful of arsenic powder and that was that. What about you?'

Anna Karenina took a while to reply. She played with a loose strand of her black hair before turning directly to Emma, a strange gleam in her eyes.

'Vengeance. Vague fury and a craving for vengeance.' She shuddered as she remembered the heavy iron blow of the train's wheel on her head. 'Revenge was more or less my final thought. Of course, I was upset and confused too but if men knew our capacity for vengeance they would tremble in their socks. Never have I hated anyone as I suddenly hated that man. Love turned to hate. I can still see his stony face when we began to quarrel. All I wanted to do was hurt him. Death was my way of reviving his love for me, punishing him and finally gaining victory in the contest.'

Emma was slightly shocked. She did not think she had it in her heart to be as ruthless as Anna. She closed Flaubert's novel and laid it on her lap.

Anna looked at her in surprise: 'Have you stopped reading? Do you not want to know what happened after you died? I do.'

Emma, with some reluctance, opened her book again and turned to the last few pages. She reached the point when her mother-in-law moved in to comfort Charles after her death.

'Oh, I see the old bat got him back after I'd gone. She was always jealous of me.'

Anna laughed. 'Vronsky's mother hated me too. He'd given up a prestigious military career for me. She adored me at first then she thought I'd ruined her son's life.'

'How do you mean?' Emma tried to hide her prurience.

The colour rose up through Anna's neck and into her cheeks at the memory.

'Well, Vronsky and I chose to live together without my being divorced. That meant we were social outcasts. We were refused invitations. Spurned by old friends. Nobody would visit us. And once I was at the opera when the wife of a couple in the next box ostentatiously rose and left rather than be seen to be sitting near me.'

For a few moments Emma was quite glad she did not move in those circles. It crossed her mind that maybe the French Revolution hadn't been such a bad thing. She read on.

'Oh it seems that Charles really did love me. He kept a lock of my hair and gave me a very grand tombstone.' Then her hand shot up to cover her mouth. 'Oh no.' She looked up in horror at Anna. 'He's found all my love letters. The ones to Leon and the ones to Rodolphe. Now he knows everything.' She continued to read. 'Shit. Now he's actually bumped into Rodolphe in the market at Argueil. This is dreadful.' She covered her face with her hands and then peeped back at the book. 'Oh and now he's died. Just as well, probably.'

Anna was studying the last pages of the Tolstoy novel with great intensity.

'Good. I'm so glad I was looking beautiful when Vronsky came to see my dead body at the train station.' She put the book down and said with sarcasm: 'I suppose we have to be thankful that Kitty and Levin carry some hope of happiness in the world.' She explained to Emma, 'Kitty couldn't get Vronsky so she had to make do with Levin. Vronsky always thought Levin was a crackpot with his communist ideas. Anyway, I got what I wanted. Vronsky rejoined the military and went off to war. He would almost certainly have been killed. At least nobody else would have him.' She snapped the book shut with triumph and offered it to Emma. 'Do you want to read it?'

'I don't think so. Not if it doesn't have a happy ending.' Emma continued to grumble about her author. 'I don't think that Flaubert could have approved of me if he gave me such an unattractive death. I like books where death is more romantic.'

'I'm not sure that Tolstoy liked me either. Anyway, apparently Tolstoy was a complete pain in the neck but look at what he created.' Anna's eyes flashed with humour and she pulled the cashmere shawl around her shoulders.

'Do you think people will remember us?' asked Emma.

'Oh yes,' said Anna, smiling. 'People will remember us more vividly than they remember their own relatives.'

Soon the women were drawn back to their respective windows. As long as they were residents in that city of waiting much of their time was spent at the window, re-living certain short but very particular moments in their lives.

THE DARK PHOTON

Even as I write, I think of the time when the pages will have turned to dust, the computers long since disintegrated and all life vanished, leaving nothing behind but the cold universe. And then the universe itself gone out. Total extinction. But I write anyway.

It was either February or March – I'm not good on dates and it was a while ago. I was staying in the Nunez area of Buenos Aires, having returned to Argentina after many years (assuming that I didn't just dream I'd returned, as it sometimes seems). Unwilling to pick up the threads of my former life I told no-one I was coming back. Instead I rented a small apartment and spent the evenings on my own, cooking for myself or eating pizza and preparing my conference paper on the dark photon – that elusive portal into the world of dark matter – which I was to present at the university later in the week. Earlier that same evening I had gone to the trouble of making a beef stew which I was mopping up with tortillas, while keeping half an eye on the television in order to catch one of the crazier soap operas.

The loud knocking on the front door of the building signalled distress. It came late at night. I looked out of the window of my fifth-floor flat. My friend Bernardo Brach, whom I had not seen for years but who was immediately recognisable, was standing on the pavement outside. I had to go down five flights of the narrow staircase because, for some reason, he refused to let me throw down the keys. The lights on the stairway didn't work. When I reached the ground floor Bernardo stood there in the glare of the street lamp. He looked more haggard than when I had last seen him in the United States. To my alarm he had a suitcase with him. He caught my disconcerted glance at his bag.

It's all right. I'm not staying. I need to ask you something then I'll be on my way.

We embraced each other and went upstairs to my flat.

How did you know I was back?

I keep an eye on what's happening. You're here for the science convention, aren't you? I saw your name and cajoled one of the secretaries into giving me your address. I've been back here myself, looking into some things . . .

His voice tailed off. The stubble on his face suggested that he had not shaved for at least two days. He was staring intensely at the floor with the closed sweaty look of a man who is living a secret life in his head.

We wasted hardly any time discussing what we had both been doing since we last saw each other. I now lived in London and worked in the physics department of Imperial College. Bernardo had settled in North America. We had been close friends at school and since then had kept in touch, if only infrequently. He told me he had worked at various jobs and tried running an unsuccessful art gallery. His own artwork was an eccentric mix of installations built from old Meccano and Lego sets combined with whatever industrial bric-a-brac caught his eye on the streets or in the boatyards of Miami, where he now lived. He never sold much but nor did he waver from his commitment to this type of work.

Bernardo had sought me out for only one reason. He wanted to know if I remembered a teacher we had at school and if I thought I would still recognise him. He paced around the room and smoked.

Did you take history at school?

Yes. Briefly.

Then you must remember him.

I did indeed remember Felipe Guzman.

In the last year of our school days I was the window monitor in charge of opening or closing the windows according to the temperature. In summer, the afternoon sun baked our stuffy classroom which smelled of wood, polish and chalk. I remember the way the cords looped down over the radiators because in winter I made sure I sat huddled next to the heating system. Our school was in the suburbs of Buenos Aires, a city which thought well of itself even in those unsettling days, a sophisticated city, the perfect mix of Europe and Latin America.

We were all impressed by the new history teacher. There was something cavalier in the way he tossed his front lock of black hair and smoothed it back with his hand as he spoke. His face had an extraordinary pallor as if he had never seen the South American sun but his lips were red and well defined. He sported a simple but impeccably stylish wardrobe consisting of a white open-necked shirt, black trousers and a waistcoat. All told, he was nothing like our other shabbier and less charismatic teachers. There were rumours about him. Who knows where these rumours came from but pupils love to speculate about the lives of their teachers outside the classroom. We knew he came from an illustrious naval family and his uncle was a hero in the national polo playing team. But they said that, for a while, he had abandoned the family to hang out with low-life petty criminals in the villas miserias; that he was the artist responsible for some notorious and shocking graffiti in the Plaza de Mayo. Maybe we just invented all that. Then there was some story about his making provocative or scandalous gestures, thumbing his nose at a high-ranking naval officer – something unheard of in those days. But, if indeed those stories were true, he was never arrested or even cautioned, perhaps because of his family's influence.

Anyway, we all admired him. The girls, in particular, adored him. But for some reason I felt that he never liked me. I had the irrational idea that it was because he once overheard me commenting on how small his feet were, dainty almost, in their shiny black shoes. Whatever the reason, I was excluded from a chosen elite of students who were permitted to mix with him out of school. There were eight or nine of them. How I longed to be part of that group. My friend Bernardo was in it. Looking back now I understand how fortunate I was to be excluded.

But at the time I was jealous of Bernardo. Whenever he came to my house after school I tried to pump him as to what happened in those get-togethers with Guzman. I could sense that he really wanted to tell me. We were good friends after all. But at the last moment he would assume the earnest look that only a seventeen-year-old can have, of one who is party to grave matters or, more hurtful, the doubtful look of one who could not trust me to keep a secret. On top of that, I resented the fact that Rosaria Bianchi, a classmate whom I dreamed of dating, also attended those meetings with Guzman, as did Javier Otero and Joaquin Ponce, all of whom had previously been part of my gang of friends and all of whom had fallen under the magnetic attraction of Felipe Guzman. One after the other he invited them to his soirees.

It would be fair to say that our sixth form had no particular interest in politics. We had the usual concerns of middle-class youngsters: worries about exams and what future career path to take; support for various sports teams – the football World Cup was being hosted in Argentina that year – and, of course, the intense friendships, sexual blossoming, rivalries and crushes which occur at that age. Those were our preoccupations. My immediate future was already determined. My father was moving the family to England where he had been offered work as an engineer and I was enrolled to study physics at London University.

Gradually, in that last school term, I noticed a change in Bernardo. There would be a quick exchange of glances between him and the other classmates in Guzman's group at any mention of the Monteneros, a guerrilla group whose revolutionary activities had been, by then, more or less extinguished – it was the late seventies. Once, to my puzzlement, he became involved in a heated discussion about the plight of some local garbage workers who were on strike.

I should mention one particular boy in our class, Alfredo Gonzales. He was short and stocky with a mop of orange hair and a broad pale freckled face, and he never stopped smiling. We felt there was something idiotic about his grin. What's more he did not look like a South American, more Scandinavian or Irish although his family had been in Argentina for generations. Unlike most of us he seemed completely open, almost as if he had been turned inside out with nothing hidden. This was both distasteful and shocking to us adolescents, fierce guardians of our own private and very secret passions. We found his openness horrifying. The other thing that we scorned was his love of folk music. He came from the area of Salta known for its traditional folk songs. His parents had saved up so that he could attend our high school and he boarded with a guardian in Buenos Aires. The man he worshipped was Jorge Cafrune, one of Salta's most famous and popular folk singers. In our opinion, Cafrune was a hick who rode around on a white horse, wearing a gaucho hat and singing crummy songs with a political message. The Stones, Led Zeppelin and David Bowie were more to our taste. But in our last year Cafrune was assassinated, deliberately run down and killed by a van in Benavidez. His horse was found disembowelled nearby, its brown satiny entrails spilled onto the asphalt road. The perpetrators were never found. Alfredo was so upset he did not come to school for three days. It must have been around then that Felipe Guzman approached him. To everyone's surprise Alfredo spurned the offer to become part of Guzman's elite little cabal. In fact, he laughed at the idea. Unable to believe that someone would turn down such an invitation, I asked him why. He just maintained that idiotic grin and shrugged.

I don't like him too much, he said, and his blue eyes shone with a sort of merriment.

This confirmed our opinion that Alfredo was a peculiar sort of fish. We allowed rumours and possibilities to grow in our heads. I can't even remember why but a conspiracy grew up and we started to follow him home from where he worked in a bicycle shop on Saturday mornings. Our teasing was innocuous and didn't seem to bother him. But then one day he vanished. He went off to buy cigarettes and none of us ever saw him again. No-one heard from him despite repeated efforts on our part to contact him. In the end we assumed he'd had enough of our jibes and gone back to Salta. We felt a little guilty but then came exams, school broke up for the last time and we forgot about Alfredo.

After school finished that year I spent a lot of time at Bernardo's house. Like all adolescents I found anyone else's family more attractive than my own and our friendship deepened at the thought of imminent separation. His family lived in an affluent part of town. We were in his bedroom trying to fix a broken Gestetner duplicating machine when Bernardo finally spilled the beans about Felipe Guzman. His room resembled any other teenager's room with posters of David Bowie and the Rolling Stones plus some large Juan Miro prints. Bernardo wanted to study art. His father, a distinguished and powerful attorney, who only emerged from his study that day to give me a nod, was adamant that his son should study law. The stand-off had gone on for months.

We set about repairing the Gestetner machine. Soon our hands were daubed with black as we struggled to mend the attachment mechanism that fastened the stencils to the inked roller. When we finished, Bernardo, embarrassed I think by his own secretiveness, told me that he needed the Gestetner because he was going to roll off and deliver some leaflets to the union leader of the striking garbage workers. Did I want to come with him? We sat side by side on his bed. Sunlight caught the wispy beginning of his moustache. I remember his grey eyes alight with determination. Feeling out of my depth I made up an excuse and declined. It was a streak of cowardice of which I've always been ashamed. He swore me to secrecy, explaining that Felipe Guzman had been enlightening them about political realities and that he now saw the world in a completely different light. Guzman taught them about Marx and Trotsky; the activities of the Tupamaros in Uruguay; how the M.I.R. was the party to support in Chile because it was more revolutionary than the Communist Party. Bernardo outlined to me his new world view. It was Felipe Guzman, he said, who gave them enough heart to become involved in politics despite dangers from the current military dictatorship.

One final event convinced me that Bernardo's life had indeed taken a different turn. I had done well in my final school exams and as a reward my father presented me with two tickets to the World Cup Final. It was Argentina versus the Netherlands, to be held in River Plate's home stadium, Estadio Monumental. I was overjoyed. I phoned Bernardo immediately to ask if he would like to come with me. To my astonishment, he hesitated and then explained.

Oh Ernesto. You won't believe this but on that Saturday my parents have been invited to the Guzman family estate for drinks in the evening. My father has been doing some legal work for Rear-Admiral Guzman's wife. I really want to go with them. I'm curious to see Felipe's family background.

I was disappointed and confused. How could anyone prefer a cocktail party to a World Cup final? In the end I took my little brother to the match and we watched with joy as Argentina beat the Netherlands 3-1.

Two days later Bernardo telephoned me. He was bubbling over with excitement.

Guess what. My father has changed his mind. I'm leaving for New York on Wednesday. I'm going for an interview at the School of Visual Arts to see if I can start in September.

How did that happen? I asked.

I think it was Mrs Guzman. When she heard that I was one of her son's students she became a bit flustered. She phoned my father the next day and lo and behold I am off to art school. I don't know how she did it.

What was it like at the Guzman's? I enquired.

It was . . . well it was . . . How can I explain? I'll tell you about it when we meet. How was the football?

But we never did meet before he left for New York. Soon afterwards I set off for England and contact with Bernardo thereafter was infrequent although the affection from our schooldays remained and I visited him once in the United States.

Although July is the beginning of our Argentine winter, the weather was still warm that year and I spent the last days of my teenage years in Buenos Aires visiting the swimming pool and helping the family to pack up and leave.

It wasn't until Bernardo was pacing around my rented flat all those years later, smoking non-stop, that I learned what had happened on the evening he visited the Guzman's house in the countryside outside Buenos Aires. As far as I remember the story went something like this.

The Guzman's imposing mansion stood at the end of an avenue lined with huge, sad trees. Bernardo, in the back of his parents' car could hardly contain his excitement at visiting the family premises where his idol and mentor had been raised. He thought it would seal a special bond between them and imagined confronting Felipe Guzman with a broad smile and saying, 'Guess where I was on Saturday evening.'

They were shown into a vast lobby. The walls were hung with old, moth-eaten tapestries depicting Goya paintings.

These were interspersed with family portraits in oils that dated back to the eighteenth century. Some of the figures emerged from such deep and dazzling blackness that the background was more compelling than the subject. Despite his new political conversion, Bernardo was thrilled and could not help being impressed.

The drawing room where the evening's entertainment took place was a red-carpeted affair with gilt chairs placed around the periphery. Several people had already arrived. A liveried servant moved among them with a tray of drinks. Rear-Admiral Guzman in full naval uniform was engaged in convivial conversation with a small group of guests. Mrs Bianca Guzman sailed forward to greet Bernardo and his parents.

Mrs Guzman, despite her overweight and spreading lower half, had a youthful spirit that showed when her face lit up with delight over one thing or another. Her white hair was casually done. She wore a blue dress whose low neck allowed her to display a sparkling necklace of amethyst and diamonds. Coming from a family of diplomats, her thoughts turned almost exclusively on dinner parties, salons, placements and, of course, guest lists which included the most prestigious luminaries she could find. She was a woman of considerable acumen and a snob of almighty proportions. Her talents as a hostess were unsurpassed. However, when she understood that Bernardo was her son's pupil, she pulled him to one side and spent a surprising amount of time with him, considering that he was the youngest and least important person there.

Apparently she questioned Bernardo as to whether he had noticed anything odd about her son. She tossed her head back and laughed:

Of course, he is something of an artist and they always do odd things. People tell me he's a brilliant photographer and film-maker. He dabbles in other genres too. We're not sure where it will all end. How do you find him?

She clasped her hands together and questioned Bernardo with a troubled smile. He could not help noticing the anxiety in her voice. Clearly she was proud of her son but Bernardo had the distinct impression that she was also frightened of him. Finally she detached herself and went to attend to her other guests.

When the party was in full swing and everyone engaged in conversation, Bernardo needed the bathroom. He asked one of the waiters where it was and slipped out. Somehow or other he must have misunderstood the directions. He went through the lobby and along a corridor. At the end of the corridor he was faced with a wide downward sloping carpeted ramp that ended in a flight of stairs leading to an underground cellar area. At the end of another narrower corridor was a door marked *Private*. Bernardo opened it. The room was dark. He thought at first it was a gymnasium. One wall was lined with wall bars. Then he thought it was a gruesome display of post-modern art. Hanging upside down from the bars was the figure of a body with the throat cut, drained of blood and with the scalp partially torn off. Next to it hung a chainsaw and an electric cattle prod. Scattered around were a few badly made plaster heads, Roman style. And in the centre of the room was a figure bound and gagged in a chair. The figure was mummified, swathed from head to foot in greying frayed bandages. An opening at the top revealed matted clumps of orange hair. The figures were models or mannequins of some sort, he thought, but he could not see properly in the dim light.

He backed out of the room. One thing he knew. He was not going to mention to Felipe Guzman that he had visited his parents' house. He found his way back up the ramp to the drawing room by following the buzz, chatter and laughter of the party.

Bernardo stood in front of me in the flat, quizzing me about our school days:

Do you remember Rosaria Bianchi from school? And the others who were in Guzman's group, little Otero and Joaquin Ponce? He asked.

Yes.

Did you know what happened to them?

No. What happened?

Bernardo opened his suitcase. It contained an old-fashioned video cassette recorder and a couple of old video tapes. He began to plug the video recorder into my TV set, explaining as he worked:

I've spent most of the last week at the Escuela Superior de Mecanica de la Armada, the old Naval Petty-Officers Mechanics School. You can probably see the building from your window here. Did you know what was going on there while we were sitting in our classroom at school?

Not at the time. None of us did, did we? I've heard since. It was a holding centre for prisoners of some sort wasn't it?

Bernardo's face twisted into a grimace.

And a torture centre. Since 2007 it's been a memorial museum. The archives have detailed records, statements, testimonies, recordings and so on. I found these tapes. Take a look.

He held up some old-fashioned video tapes then inserted one into the device.

Grainy black and white pictures appeared on my TV screen. There were scenes of young people dancing.

Do you recognise anyone?

I squinted at the screen. Bernardo pressed 'pause' and froze the picture:

Don't you think that is Rosaria Bianchi who was in our class?

The face of the young girl with a mass of brown curls was turned slightly away from the camera.

It could be, I said.

Bernardo was ejecting one video tape and replacing it with another.

Now see this.

I noticed his hands were shaking. This video tape was in colour. The first rather unsteady shot was of an open aeroplane door through which could be seen, far below, what looked like a sheet of brilliant blue glass. Superimposed on the tape in hand-written script were the words Lago Buenos Aires, Patagonia, 12th November, 1978. The camera tilted and some mountains at the edge of the lake came briefly into view. Then the camera turned to the interior of the plane focusing on a burly man in a brown leather airman's jacket. He was man-handling a young boy whose eyes were half-closed towards the open door of the plane. Wind blew the boy's hair back as he was shoved out into empty space, arms and legs splaying as he fell. The roar of the engine continued as the plane moved on. It was a military plane without seats, just an empty hold. The camera turned to show maybe a dozen more bodies sitting or lying slumped against one another. The man reached down to the nearest girl and dragged her to the door. She put up some feeble resistance, holding weakly on to the sides of the plane before being kicked in the back and catapulted into the void.

Bernardo froze the tape. He took a deep breath.

I have all the records. Everything is there, the names of the torturers, which times they tortured, who was present. Young left-wing activists, including Guzman's group from our school, were arrested, tortured and held at the Naval Mechanics School. Lively music was played and they were instructed to dance for joy because they were going to be transferred south to another location where they would be better treated and from there released. Then they were injected with pentathol, having been told it was a vaccination against typhus. When they became drowsy they were loaded onto a truck and taken to the airfield. Then they were thrown out of the plane at about fourteen thousand feet, over that lake or over the Rio del Plato or sometimes out into the Atlantic Ocean. It happened on a regular basis, every other week, on a Wednesday, some-times fifteen or twenty victims at a time. There were around two hundred death flights between 1977 and 1978. It was President Videla's preferred method – he thought that Argen-tinian society would never endure firing squads. When incriminating bodies were washed up later from the Rio del Plato, one officer remarked 'We should have thrown them into a volcano.'

Now watch this.

He pressed 'play'.

The video continued. There came the sound of a voice saying what sounded like 'My turn.' The words were barely audible over the deafening roar of the engines. The camera changed hands. A second man with his back to the camera was hauling a girl by her hair. She seemed semi-conscious. He tipped her out of the plane. The wind blew her skirt up over her head as she slowly somersaulted into the sky. There was the sound of laughter. The plane roared on. The man turned round and smiled at the camera. His smooth black hair was blown back by the wind. It was Felipe Guzman.

Bernardo turned and saw the shock on my face. He clenched his teeth and shook his head as he spoke:

How could we have been so gullible? What a gang of serious fools. We were walking along the rim of an abyss without knowing it. Guzman's mother knew. That's why she told my father to get me out of the country so quickly. Guzman dressed in the persona of David Bowie's Thin White Duke. We thought it stylish. The Thin White Duke was Bowie's fascist phase, the period when he said that Britain could do with a fascist leader. Worse still . . . I think the figure bound and gagged in the cellar was not a dummy.

There was a click in Bernardo's throat.

I think it was Alfredo Gonzales, our classmate.

I stayed where I was on a chair by the table as he continued.

Felipe Guzman's name figures in many of the torture reports. He was quoted saying, 'Yes. We threw them out just to see if they would bounce.' When the military dictatorship was over they arrested him, but he was released on a technicality. After that there was no trace of him. Then came news of his death. A letter, written by him, was discovered. A suicide note. His parents built a memorial to him in the grounds of their estate and gradually the memory of him has slipped into the past.

Bernardo had the same earnest look in his eyes that I remembered from our schooldays.

The reason I'm here is because word has it that Felipe Guzman is not dead at all. He is in England. That's why I've come to you. I have an address. We need someone who could recognise him.

My stomach churned. I wanted nothing to do with all this. I wanted to get on quietly with my work.

I can't just turn up and knock on a door. What would I do then?

All we want is someone to identify him for certain. We tracked him to Japan. And some years later he spent time in Australia. Then he vanished. It seems he's re-appeared in London. I'm told that he now owns a popular Latin American restaurant. This man, if it is him, spends nearly every night there. You wouldn't have to knock on any door. You would just need to go there and take a look. Verify that it's him.

Who is this 'we' you're talking about?

Bernardo started packing up the tapes and equipment.

Just me and someone who has an interest in tracking down those people.

What will you do if it is him? Why don't you just report it to the British police or Interpol or somebody?

I want to be absolutely sure that it's him. That's why. Then maybe . . . we'll tell the police. Will you do it?

My heart sank.

Well, I'll see. I'll try. But it's a long time ago. Over thirty years. He might not look the same. Perhaps he's changed. Perhaps he's reformed.

People don't change.

Bernardo was ready to leave. He grasped my arms:

Try. Will you at least try?

Ok.

We embraced and he went downstairs. I watched from the window as he made his way down the street. From where I stood I could see the roof of the Naval Mechanics School in the park, a colonnaded building, the white top just visible over the waving ocean of dark trees.

I went to sit at my desk away from the window. Working on my paper seemed the only way to blot out what I had just heard and seen. I took out my laptop and concentrated. The work was not original research on my part. It was a matter of evaluating the latest experiments in the search for the dark photon. The trouble is that no-one has been able to discover this particle. Over many years experiments have been undertaken, often underground where there is less interference; in a deep mine in South Dakota; in a tunnel beneath mountains in northern Italy; in a huge subterranean structure beneath the South Pole: even in the CERN Hadron Collider. The search continues. After all, the Higgs-Boson particle eventually allowed itself to be revealed.

It was a relief to work late into the night. My concluding paragraphs illustrated the fact that all the experiments had so far proved fruitless. Something we cannot see and maybe cannot know is at work. Dark matter. Dark energy. An invisible force. Whatever we choose to call it. I finished the paper by explaining that we are none the wiser as to the dark photon. The current state of play is that we are unsure that it even exists. I ended with a joke about known unknowns.

It was nearly two o'clock in the morning when I finished my paper and shut the laptop. I was tired but pleased to have put some distance between myself and Bernardo's visit. Something had been achieved, at least. For some reason I remembered that day in Bernardo's house when he asked me to go with him to deliver pamphlets and I turned him down. I don't doubt that it is a form of cowardice that I recognise in myself.

I have always been wary of sticking my neck out and in my heart of hearts I knew, almost as soon as he asked me, that I would not carry out Bernardo's request when I returned to England.

A FABLE OF TALES UNTOLD

I am now in my eighties and still trying. Lucky to be here at
all, I suppose.

Then, I was thirteen and near to tears. My mother was
attempting to lengthen my short trousers. She sat on the bunk
with pins in her mouth undoing the hems of the trouser legs and
fretting over where she could find enough material to make
them into full length trousers. No-one in the dormitory below
had been able to provide her with enough suitable cloth. The
trousers looked ridiculous. But it was not only because of the
trousers that I was tearful. My voice had broken. Overnight my
voice had become gruff, squeaky and unreliable and I had been
thrown out of Bundibar, the children's opera. The opera was
popular. Sometimes we were even filmed – for propaganda
purposes, I learned later. We used to perform regularly to packed
houses and I loved being in it. But I could no longer sing. That
meant that I would not qualify for the extra rations given to the
children's choir. Worse, from my point of view, I would be cut
off from my friends. Particularly Iveta. I had a crush on her and
fell asleep every night imagining I rescued her from unspeakable
dangers. Of course, I did not know of the real dangers that

surrounded us. I'm not sure that any of us children fully under-stood. Although we knew enough to dread the arrival of the guards with a slip of paper that meant you and your family were on the transport list and would be transferred to goodness knows where, our fragile friendship networks torn apart.

I kicked up a fuss about my short trousers. If I am no longer a child, I want long trousers, I yelled at my helpless mother. I mooched about the camp. Eventually my mother managed to swap turnips and potatoes from the kitchen garden where she worked for cuttings from the leather workshop. She cut and stitched and sewed as best she could. There was no light from our small attic window because it was covered with blackout paper, so she worked by candlelight. Eventually, she held up the patched leather trousers in triumph and I graduated into long trousers.

The camp at Theresienstadt was a showcase concentration camp, if such a thing can be imagined. Terezin was a fortress town about thirty miles from Prague with a walled garrison. The camp was designed to fool the Red Cross as to how well we were being treated. And, indeed, when the Red Cross came they thought it was a self-regulating Jewish community. Jewish scholars, professionals, artists and musicians were sent there. It was part camp, part ghetto. Propaganda films announced that Hitler had given the Jews a city to themselves. In some ways it did resemble any other Jewish ghetto – apart from the guards, of course. There were armed guards. SS guards watched as musicians played in a bandstand in the square. There were lectures where the guards dozed at the back. There was a central library and cultural performances with guards always in attendance. My family was privileged because my father was a well-known mathematician. So my parents, my sister and I were allocated a cramped but private cubby-hole in the attic above a dormitory which housed about forty people.

It turned out that my exit from the children's opera was a blessing. I spent time in the library. There I found my vocation. I wrote stories and discovered that I wanted nothing else than to be a writer, a conviction that stays with me to this day. I wrote tirelessly in lined exercise books. I proudly signed each story: Max Ginz. The books were scarce so I wrote in tiny writing all over the pages, round the edges and up and down the margins. Of course, the stories mainly featured Iveta and involved a lot of sorcerers and spells but over the next couple of years I began to write descriptions of the life around me too, the black rotten potatoes we ate, the mouldy bread, the meagre rations and the transport lists, those disappearances that left a neighbouring room previously full of a noisy family suddenly empty with a few scattered belongings discarded because they would not fit into the one suitcase permitted.

The day came when my father climbed the wooden stairs to our attic quarters pale and breathless.

Max, what is in these notebooks of yours?

I had left my exercise books in a pile on a shelf under the library window because there was too little space in our attic cubby-hole. I looked at my father's worried face.

Just my stories. I write stories.

The guards have found your stories. He bent down and took my hands in his. His eyes were anxious behind those precious glasses that I noticed now had a cracked lens.

Max. Soon we hope the war will be over and then you will be able to write all the stories you want. But for now you must stop. The guards threaten to put us on the list. I'm sorry, but this has to stop.

I was horrified and frightened. I never set foot in the library again. At night I continued writing in my head. In May, 1945 the camp was liberated. One day the SS guards just disappeared. We hardly realised and continued for a day or so with the normal routine until the Soviet Army turned up and then we understood that we had indeed been liberated. We emerged dazed into the outside world and returned to Prague, lucky to be alive.

My father was right. Under the Soviet occupation I was able to write all the stories I wanted. But I could not get them published. For twenty years my writing remained a parallel life to the one in which I graduated, married, worked and fathered a son. I wrote at night in our shabby apartment in Zizkov. In the daytime I taught at a school in the neighbouring district of Vinohrady. To secure that job I had been obliged to join the Communist Party. Manuscript after manuscript was submitted to the state-controlled publishers. They were always sent back with the same note saying they did not fit in with the publisher's editorial policy. In an attempt to find the root of the problem I managed to secure an interview with one of the bureaucrats in the Ministry of Culture. The middle-aged woman sitting behind the desk had a round face smooth and white as fungus with a few brown spots. A shaft of light from the high window behind her made the crown of her chestnut hair shine. To my surprise she seemed sympathetic.

I'm sorry. I read it and liked it very much. She sighed and closed the folder with my latest submission. Then she pushed it across the desk towards me and pointed to the handwritten note attached to it. The words 'We find this work harmful to socialism' were scrawled across it.

She shook her head and shrugged to show that there was nothing she could do. I smiled and tried to persuade her otherwise.

You know literature shouldn't really serve any ideology. It touches what is in each one of us, what makes us resemble one another. It resists all systems. Isn't there anyone else in authority who could—?

But the woman had closed up and was gathering her papers together.

Several years later the Prague Spring provided unexpected hope. Even after it was crushed something in us had changed. Suddenly we found the shrill government propaganda, which nobody believed, hilarious. Quite often we were reduced to tears of laughter at the official optimism on television as smiling tractor drivers and prize-winning factories appeared on the screen. We writers found the courage to pass round samizdat copies of our work. Small groups of us gathered in secret to read them. For the first time I had some response to my efforts. People were enthusiastic. My work was popular and highly praised. Word spread and I had requests from several groups to come and read at their gatherings.

One day a visitor turned up at our place. He was a fresh-faced young man with blond wavy hair who had been at one of my readings a year or so before. I remembered him because he had talked with intelligence about my writing. He explained that he wanted to be a poet and was desperate to find work that allowed him time to write and think. He admired my work and was curious to know what I had written recently. I brought out the latest sheaves of paper and we laughed together at the satirical passages about our daily life in Prague.

125

A week later I came home from school to find my wife shaking with fear.

The police have been here.

The Secret Police had invaded our apartment searching for illegal literature. The young man might have been a poet. He was also a police informer. My wife sat with her head in her hands. I had not meant to cause her this sort of anguish.

That same week I was expelled from the Communist Party, sacked from my teaching job and branded a class enemy of the working people. Fortunately, my wife kept her job as an administrator at the Hotel Diplomat and that kept us afloat until I could find other work. For some reason, in her quiet way, she still supported me.

Of course you must go on writing. But now we must find somewhere safe to keep your work.

I loved her for that. We knew we were probably being watched. We checked regularly for bugs planted in the house. Finally, I found a menial job in an industrial laundry that dealt with sheets and bedding from all the hotels and hospitals in the district. It meant that my hands were permanently red and wrinkled from hooking swathes of cloth out of the cylindrical boiling vats and my face had a near permanent shine from exposure to the steam. I came home with my damp clothes stinking of sweat and cheap bleach. But all the same we would embrace with affection in the evening before I sat down to eat sausage and tomatoes. Then I would go into the next room and sit in front of my typewriter. If I was too tired I would watch television with my wife and son.

My wife watched as my hair grew first grey at the temples and then white as the years passed. Occasionally I had a cull and went through my work throwing out anything I considered below standard. But I continued writing. I wrote plays that I knew would never see the light of day. I wrote poetry that no-one would ever read. I wrote novels that would never be published. I always tried to make them as good as possible. I could struggle for hours changing the word 'the' to 'a' and back again trying to find the most precise expression of what I wanted to say. It was my private pleasure.

No-one saw it coming. I certainly did not.

It was November, 1989. There had been skirmishes throughout the city and then a few days later millions of citizens took to the streets, a spring tidal flood of citizenry: medical workers in their white coats, printers, drivers, workers from the factories; this huge river of people spilled out from some unidentifiable source and poured through the streets of Prague. A new city became visible that the day before had been unseen. Truckloads of students waving our red, blue and white flags roared through the streets. Holding hands, my wife, son and I joined the jubilant crowds in Wenceslas Square. Under the grey skies we were blinking as if we had just emerged into the light of day.

After the collapse of the regime things began to look up. Within a week my son found work at the Barrandov film studios. I had reached retiring age from the laundry but my wife still worked at the Hotel Diplomat. One day, soon after our velvet revolution, she came home from work and as she prepared our supper in the kitchen she described with qualified amusement what she had observed that morning:

You should have seen them. There were noisy German business men all over the restaurant area having what they call working breakfasts. One guy was given a contract for five hundred new police stations. Another man was banging his fist on the table so that his muesli jumped up and down. He was trying to persuade some government official to give him the contract to build all the new public toilets in the city. Envelopes stuffed with money were changing hands.

She dropped some dumplings into the soup and paused.

We should warn the Kramars. Someone is trying to buy half the real estate in Jecna Street. They could be turfed out.

But, apart from worries about the Kramars and other friends, I found it all refreshing. Freedom at last.

Within a year numerous new publishing houses were set up. I went to see one of them. We talked in an open plan office full of light. The two editors were enthusiastic about my work. A bright girl with spiky plum-coloured hair smiled at me.

We loved it. But we have to take account of the projected sales figures. Marketing is the problem. Unfortunately, we couldn't persuade our sales team that it was worth investing in you. They thought the work was great but wouldn't sell. She raised her hands in despair.

It was the same everywhere. All the publishers regretted that they could not publish my work – as they would wish – because it was not marketable. This gnawed at my guts. I had survived two totalitarian systems and emerged intact. I could no longer blame the evils of fascism, the oppression of Soviet communism. This so-called freedom was just a different, more insidious form of suffocation. Now for the first time the finger of blame was pointed at me. The lack of publication was my fault, not the fault of the system. I was not up to the mark, not popular enough. It was the most cunning means of extinction. Everyone that I met was warm, friendly and enthusiastic about my work. They reminded me of the sympathetic priests who accompany a man to the execution chamber.

At home I continued to write. But now I saw life around me as a gross deception under the banner of freedom. A hideous distortion. So I wrote about that. Our democracy was not freedom at all. It was a pleasant mask over an ugly system. In those other times it was clear that we were not free. Now we believed we were free but were being deceived. Our freedom was a chimera. I was enraged.

Eventually, as a last resort, I took my novel to an elderly Jewish publisher in Mala Strana. It was a small outfit dedicated to publishing Jewish material, mostly but not always by Jewish authors. We sat in his office overlooking the olive waters of the Vltava. Outside, the wind was making herringbone patterns on the surface of the river below. On Karlov Bridge a group of children played happily around a life-size figure wearing a Mickey Mouse costume. The editor-in-chief looked at me seriously over his desk, a small wizened man wearing a crocheted skull cap:

Look out of the window, Mr Grinz, and tell me that those children playing there would have been better off under the Nazis, or the Soviet communists. Have you not thought about what you are saying here? That the freedoms you have now are not worth it – that they are a sort of unfreedom worse for you than being in a concentration camp? He stared at me with hostility and for a moment I was distracted by his spectacles, one lens of which was chipped just as my father's had been. He shook his head: I ask you to reconsider, Mr Ginz. We could not publish this. What you are saying here is a blasphemy. An outrage. How can you think that this life is worse? He closed up my manuscript and handed it back to me over the table.

The trouble was, I thought, as I walked downhill through the steep cobbled streets of the old town, that I did think this life for a writer was worse. It felt so to me because rejection on account of marketability made it personal. I could no longer blame the system. At one time I could hold up two fingers to the Nazi system or the Communist system. Now I had to hold up two fingers to myself. It was my fault.

Already an idea for a new story was forming in my head.

LET ME OUT

He was small, enigmatic and bright. My first encounter with him was on the day I started work in the foundry. A holiday job. As a student I wanted to earn money for an Inter-rail ticket to Europe. The business was a small concern amongst ramshackle workshops and scrap metal firms on an industrial estate in Yarmouth where I lived. They fashioned metal sculptures and various other works of art. I arrived early on that first day. The L-shaped building was surprisingly clean and airy, full of light with white-painted walls. There was no-one else there except a man whom I took to be some sort of janitor or watchman. He was perched on one of the tables. He had a small sharp face and his black clothes had an old-fashioned look. They were too big for him. He seemed to have taken it upon himself to give me instructions.

In front of me stood a bucket of soapy water.

'Ye just wash him down fust,' he instructed, 'with a clean cloth.' His head was cocked to one side. 'Like ye might do a corpse, before ye lay it out.' He chuckled and looked to see my reaction.

The bronze statue was laid out on a long table in front of me. It did, indeed, look like a huge metal corpse. A politician or dignitary of some sort. No-one I recognised. I started cleaning one leg, tentatively.

'Go on. Give it some welly.' His manner was cocky. 'D'ye know where that saying comes from? The Duke of Wellington. Give it some welly. Some power. A bit of elbow grease.'

I scrubbed away.

'That wax on him, you'll have to take it all off. That's the last thing they do when they're making a bronze statue. Give him a coat of wax. Then the air and humidity can't turn him green, d'ye see? Oxidisation. I know it all. Been there. Done that.'

He slid off the table and took a step forward to examine the figure.

'But this chap, the patina has worn off and he's looking a bit mouldy. When ye get to the fiddly bits ye might need a soft toothbrush to get in the nooks and crannies, clean off the bird droppings. There are some old toothbrushes in a jar over there.'

He wandered off, calling back:

'When ye're done ye'll need to wipe him down with clean water to get rid of the soap residue. Then give him a couple of hours to dry. He has to dry completely because he'll need to be re-waxed and we don't want to trap any moisture underneath.'

He turned back at the door grinning.

'How dead are the dead? That's what we need to know, eh?'

The foundry manager came in to find me already at work. He was a solid, balding man who wore a navy canvas apron and moved with particular lightness on his feet. His private passion was pottery and he had a potter's wheel around the corner where he worked when he was not busy on the sculptures. He was surprised that I had already started work and knew what to do.

'Oh, you've met Ernie, have you? He's a bit of a joke here. He drops in now and then. Tells people what's what. He doesn't work here. I never see him. He keeps out of my way in case I tell him to mind his own business. Fancy you bumping into him on your first day.'

He ran his hand over the statue to make sure the wax had been properly cleaned off.

As it happened, I was grateful for Ernie's advice. It saved me making mistakes and losing time. I could see him through the window outside the adjoining outfit where they recycled used car tires. He was in front of a wall leaning against a stack of old tyres writing something on a sheaf of papers. On top of the wall behind him a black cat was licking itself. Later on I discovered that he was full of odd bits of information, an autodidact who had picked up scraps of random knowledge through his trade – whatever his trade might have been.

'Sennacherib.' He said one time when I was sweeping up. 'Ever heard of him? Ancient Assyrian. Wolf on the fold. Claimed to be the first to make a bronze statue. A curse on him for that.'

The atmosphere in the foundry was relaxed. Not many people worked there. The few employees sauntered about casually with caked plaster on their jeans or aprons, setting about their various tasks. They were sculptors and craftsmen, some part-time, each with his own interest. No-one explained much to me. I was the general dogsbody.

Three or four days after I started a sculptor arrived with a model that was to be transformed into a statue. It was the life-size figure of a soldier for a local war memorial in Yarmouth. The first stage was to make a rubber mould and cast a wax copy. Ernie came up behind me. He spoke with some distaste as the men struggled with the slithery rubber mould:

'See that mould. It's all floppy and flexible, a giggling un-controllable sort of thing.' Ernie shuddered with dislike. 'Nobody would like to see themselves like that. It's humiliat-ing. That would embarrass anybody, seeing a rubber mould of themselves wobbling all over. Especially a military man.'

Two men poured hot wax into the mould as I watched. Later when the wax had solidified, Ernie muttered in my ear:

'He'll be dismembered now. Divided into sections for firing in the kiln. I don't like to see this.'

The soldier was laid out on one of the long tables and I was astonished to see how exactly every last detail was reproduced in the wax model, down to the broad nose, the fine strands of hair and the defiant expression on his face. Once the wax had set one of the workmen took a large knife and cut into the throat. The knife slid through the soft wax severing the head. I had a feeling of horror as the head came away. I looked round. Ernie had gone. The rest of the figure was routinely dissected, the limbs and torso placed separately on the table.

The boss came up to me:

'All right, lad, you can help with this next bit now.'

Soon I was in an apron and up to my elbows in the wet, heat-resistant plaster which we packed round the divided sections of the figure. When the plaster had set, the men stacked the sections in the kiln. Then they shut the kiln door and fired the kiln.

Ernie appeared when I was standing at the sink with my arms under the tap washing off the plaster before it congealed.

'There's a thought,' he said. 'He'll be locked in there for five days at a temperature of six hundred degrees centigrade until the wax is vaporised. They have to go through every stage of the inferno these people. This wasn't the sort of after-life they were expecting, eh?'

There was something odd about Ernie. His age was indeterminate and he seemed to spring out of nowhere in his long black coat, as if someone's shadow had torn itself away and burst into a three-dimensional life of its own. The inquisitive blue eyes in his small face were always following me about. He had taken a liking to me and cornered me to bend my ear when no-one else was around.

'They brought Friedrich Engels back to Manchester. He was abandoned in Poltava in Eastern Ukraine. Concrete. All covered in lichen. It would be a mistake to think that all those abandoned statues lack power.' He wandered over to look at a plaster replica of the Venus de Milo standing by the door. 'The French understood that. They beheaded the statues of their kings in the French Revolution. And there's a marble statue of Queen Victoria forsaken in the tropics somewhere, shoved there during a political upheaval, her nose broken off so the surface is all pitted and rough. But she still exerts some mysterious power over the surrounding foliage. Oh yes.' He looked thoughtful. 'They all host living forces, y'know.'

A few days later I sat outside in the sunshine eating my sandwiches. The bronze pouring was to take place that day. I had been told I could watch but I must keep well away for fear of being splashed with the incandescent liquid. The morning had been spent putting the plaster moulds into the pit. When I went back the foundry boss had changed his clothes. He and another workman now wore protective clothing, leather gaiters, spats, long thick leather gloves and full-face protective visors. I stood by the doorway and watched as they loaded the bronze ingots into the crucible and then into the furnace. They used pouring shanks to lift the crucible out again, a long metal rod with square handles at each end, like the handlebars on a bike. In the centre was the circular grip for the pot. As they lifted the crucible out of the furnace its outer surface glowed crimson with the heat from the molten bronze inside. I could feel the heat from where I stood. They staggered over to the pit, one at each end of the pole, the scorching liquid bronze skimming the edge of the pot. There, with great skill they tipped the crucible and guided the bright yellow stream of scalding bronze into the plaster moulds.

Ernie was suddenly next to me in the doorway, wiping his forehead with a large handkerchief:

'That's him in the inferno. Poor soul. Molten fury. Pure molten rage in 'im. It'll tek 'im twenty-four hours or so to cool down. Then you'll have to chip away the plaster casting and let him breathe again,' he said, before folding his handkerchief and heading outside.

Ernie was beginning to irritate me with his bits of information. He had button-holed me one day to lecture me about the difference between marble and bronze statues.

'It's the bronze ones that have all the anger. Look and ye'll see it. The marble ones are milder, more malleable, softer in appearance. They've been released y'see from blocks of marble or stone. The bronze ones have been messed about, hacked, burnt, dismembered, welded together again. There's a rage and fury in them, even in the ones that seem to be smiling. Look close and ye'll see it. The smile in't no more than a grimace, an attempt to conceal all that pain.'

He walked away, his coat flaring behind him as he went.

I wanted to shake Ernie off. I found myself deliberately staying closer to the other workmen so that he couldn't find me on my own.

The next day when the bronze had cooled I was ordered to help knock away the plaster to reveal the figure inside which was still in separate pieces. One man worked with an axe. I laboured alongside him with a hammer and chisel until parts of the figure gradually emerged from the mounting pile of plaster rubble around our feet. The powdery white plaster dust made me sneeze. When all the sections were free the soldier came out in pieces, looking rougher than I had expected. Fragments of plaster still stuck to his face. He appeared different. Instead of the bold creature the artist had brought in the soldier now looked troubled and distracted, as if he were frowning. I mentioned this to the boss.

'It will come good, you'll see,' he said, wiping his hands on his apron. 'We'll weld the sections together with a TIG welder and Silicon Bronze welding rods and then the sculptor will come back and do a bit of fettling. It's often those fine touches at the end that brings them back to life.'

And so they did. When the sculptor came back he worked on details and added touches that re-humanised the work. Under his careful hands the soldier became more relaxed. But not completely. His mouth still had a fixed rigour of tension and wariness that had not been there before.

It was my last day. My four weeks at the foundry were over. Pay packet in my pocket, I was all set to travel to Europe. Just as I was leaving the industrial estate for good Ernie came hurrying after me. I hadn't seen him for a while. He caught up with me:

'Are ye off, lad?' His sharp eyes fixed me with that penetrating stare. The collar of his black coat stood up round his neck although it was a hot day and he still had that odd metallic smell from the foundry. He took hold of my jacket sleeve: 'Have ye learned something here? I hope so. Ye'll need to study them statues more carefully now, eh? Mustn't ignore them.'

He fidgeted for a moment before suddenly erupting with anger.

'Don't ye think it's disgusting, eh? That the spirit should be locked up in that way? Locked in all that unyielding metal. For hundreds of years. That's how long statues can last, y'know. How would you like it? They've gone through every circle of the inferno, they have, from the molten rage to the frozen fury. Did ye know that the last and deepest level of Dante's inferno is not fire but ice? That's them. Pent up in ice. Benumbed. Frozen. Paralysed. Frigid. Petrified. All those trapped desires inside. And everybody scurrying by, ignoring them. No-one talks of the relief that Ozymandias felt when the sands began to erode and free him. Set him free.'

I was standing by the gate, embarrassed by the outburst and not knowing how to get away.

'Straddling life and death is tiring, mate. Believe you me. Hanging halfway between the two. But mark my words, their day will come. Just think of it. One day ye'll hear that jarring grating clank as they lever themselves off their pedestals, all those equestrian bronze statues of kings and generals facing the Houses of Parliament, horses rearing in a wild cavalry charge against the living bastards.' He shook his fist in the air with triumph. 'And all those anonymous soldiers getting off their war memorials to join them in an infantry charge. Fixed bayonets. Oh, there's some power in them yet. They want a war. D'ye know why? It's their best chance of being destroyed. All statues are angry. Pent-up spirits. They want to be smashed up.

That way the spirit is released into the air and can find its way into a living person and live again. That's what the statues want. Not any halfway house. Freedom to inhabit the living. Smash us up, they say. Set us free.'

He spat on the ground, shook his head and with shoulders hunched he turned away towards the foundry without so much as a goodbye.

I was pleased to be on my way.

All the pleasures of Europe were ahead of me. Or should have been. I had just completed my first year at university studying Italian and German. My intention was to visit Italy first and then go north to Germany, brushing up my language skills as I went. I was excited about this trip. At first I had been going to travel with friends but in the end we couldn't agree on routes and destinations so I decided to go on my own. I would arrive in London in the afternoon, catch the night train from St Pancras to Paris and travel from there direct to Florence.

I arrived in London and decided to make my way along the Thames embankment. It was difficult for me to shake off Ernie's warning that I should pay close heed to statues. I tried to ignore them but each one I passed seemed to press its attention on me. By dusk I was walking past the Houses of Parliament. Placed around Parliament Square a gruesome collection of figures awaited me immobile and silent as if in a gigantic sulk. A vagrant lay hunched in his sleeping bag at the foot of George Canning's plinth. For a moment I thought I saw the statue's face twitch. On closer inspection I saw that the statue was overrun with mice. I walked on to Victoria Station and caught the tube to St Pancras.

As soon as the train left St Pancras I experienced a sense of liberation. My anxiety fell away. We arrived at the Gare du Nord early in the morning where I had to scramble for my connection to Florence. I dozed and woke as we drew into Florence. It was four in the afternoon. I held my breath as I looked through the train window to see the great rust-coloured dome of the city's cathedral against a hazy bluish backdrop of Tuscan hills. The hotel I had booked was small and serviceable. I left my bags there and straightaway ventured out to enjoy a bowl of coffee, soft bread twists, Parma ham and olives. This was life in Italy as I had imagined it.

My sense of elation did not last long. The next morning I dutifully joined other tourists to see the iconic statue of Michaelangelo's David. The marble figure was benign and beautiful. From below I could not see whether the convoluted carving around the top of the head represented curly hair or some sort of laurel wreath. I took out my binoculars to get a better look. Immediately I was paralysed with shock. From below the face had seemed mild and tender. But as I looked through the binoculars the expression on the face changed. In close-up the face assumed such an unmistakeable expression of fear and dread that my heart went into palpitations and I fled back to my lodgings.

By the next day I seemed to have contracted some sort of virus. I was plagued with fever, headaches and a migraine which affected my vision. The migraine started by blacking out one half of the sight in my right eye. This was followed by nausea and brilliant zig-zag patterns in the eye. I pulled the shutters in my room so that it was dark and for the next few days I only left there to creep out in the evening for a snack in a nearby café before crawling back to bed. Most of my planned stay in Italy was spent under the bedcovers trying to shield myself from the light, although I did manage to go out and send a postcard to my mother in Yarmouth.

Five days later, still with fever and disappointed that I had wasted so much of the time left on my student rail card, I headed north to Munich. From there I would travel to Cologne where I had arranged to meet a friend from university. We were to meet in the large square in front of the cathedral. The two giant spires of that great Gothic church towered above me, blackened with grime. People came and went. I checked the time. Pigeons fluttered. I sat and waited in the square for an hour and a half. My phone buzzed with a text message. It was from my friend:

Sorry. I am stuck in Bamberg. Is there any chance you could come here?

As I held up my phone to read the message the bells of the cathedral suddenly boomed out behind me, over fifty-six tons of bronze metal ringing out an industrial warning with no melody. Overwhelmed by the noise I stayed pinioned to the stone seat. The famous free-swinging bronze bell that weighs twenty-four tons resonated in my ears. It was a deafening, ominous sound designed to raise the beast. The deep clanging unnerved me. It seemed to come from the bowels of the church rather than the bell tower. Eventually, the bells stopped. Then, from inside, came the long low animal growl of the church organ followed by a spray of peals like mad laughter. I scurried out of the square, messaging my friend as I went: *On my way.*

At the station I bought a ticket to Bamberg even though it was not on my schedule. I felt exhausted. My shirt was damp with sweat. I was re-tracing my steps, going back in the wrong direction from what should have been my homeward bound journey. After what seemed like a short time, I stepped off the train in the small southern town of Bamberg.

I texted my friend: *Where are you?*

A few minutes later I received a text from him: *I'm in Cologne, waiting for you. I've been here for hours. What happened?*

There is no doubt that I was unwell and in a state of confusion but how could I have made such a mistake? Tears came into my eyes. I felt bewildered and sick. There was a five-hour wait for the next train back to Cologne. I left the station and wandered aimlessly around town. After half an hour I found myself in a neat, prosperous, well-proportioned square. I remember the name. It was Schillerplatz. The house fronts were painted in pastel colours and, perhaps because I was hungry, I imagined that behind those doors were parlours and pantries stocked with sausages, sauerkraut, cream buns and pastries. It reminded me of the town of Hamelin, staid and conservative, populated with stolid citizens who slept well at night, unaware of the stars or a comet moving overhead.

In the middle of the square stood a statue, a figure, all in black, like some unspoken secret. It was neither large nor imposing, less than life-size and standing on a small plinth. Sight of the figure caused systolic and diastolic thumps of my heart to pound in my ears. My mouth went dry. I recognised him immediately. As well as the familiar long black coat, he now wore an enormous top hat, the sort of hat fashionable in the eighteenth century, wider at the top than the bottom. His clothes seemed to dwarf him. The collar rising up around his neck and the hat pulled down over his forehead almost obscured his tiny face. But when I approached I stared directly into the frozen unmistakeable features of Ernie, the man I had mistaken for the janitor at the foundry. His eyes stared back at me from a face both innocent and sinister but with an element of fury. On his right shoulder was a cat, held there by a rigid hand. In the other hand he held a manuscript.

On the plinth his name was engraved. E.T.A. Hoffmann. It was Ernst Hoffmann.

I have no memory of what happened to me immediately afterwards. I was discovered that night wandering nearby. The small private clinic that admitted me overlooked the very same square where the statue stood. At night I kept my hands over my ears to block out the sound of groans outside and the screeching of metal as he wrenched himself off the plinth and I shut my eyes. I knew he would be at my window mouthing the words *let me out*.

I was no longer able to speak. It was as if there was a metal horse's bit gagging my tongue. At night I imagined that whenever I opened my mouth metal would come clattering out: tongs, forks, those brass pans kept in the hearth for sweeping ash and embers. Gongs and cymbals. Pins, nails, metal hoops. The tangy taste of metal filled my mouth day and night.

The staff were kind and helpful. I told them over and over again to get rid of the statue outside and then I would be well. They called for my mother to come over from England and collect me.

'She will be here on Tuesday,' they said.

MORNE JALOUX

The plane tilted to make its landing approach. I watched as the brown island slanted into view and the dark blue of the Caribbean Sea shaded into the familiar pale turquoise waves breaking on the shoreline. A prickle of anxiety ran along my arms and up the nape of my neck. The nervousness had nothing to do with the landing. It had to do with the visit. I reassured myself that in twenty-four hours I would be leaving again.

I had not set foot on the island for twenty-five years. There was a blast of hot air as I stepped out onto the plane steps. This airport was new to me. When I was last on the island it had been under construction in the blazing sun with Cuban engineers consulting their plans and Cuban guest-workers struggling to shift blocks of cement, their bare backs gleaming in the sun. In those days I had flown into the old airport to be greeted by two smiling members of the new revolutionary government.

Now I shuffled along the slow line towards the passport desk. Two customs officials leant against the wall. They looked relaxed but for me there was the sense of a bad dream, as if, behind the wall, dogs were waiting to be released or the sudden sound of gunfire and screams might be heard and bloodstains appear on the floor.

The woman at passport control fingered my passport.

'How long are you staying?'

'One day.'

Her face expressed surprise and disapproval as if the brevity of my stay was a personal insult.

'Purpose of visit?'

'Er . . . visiting friends'.

I had no clear idea myself why I was there or what had compelled me to return.

The taxi took me through a terrain of bare brown hills dotted with wooden shacks. The island felt dead and sullen as if it had never recovered from those brutal internecine events. Eventually the capital came into view elegantly draped over the cliff side and along the bay.

I had booked into a luxury hotel on the beach. A professionally smiling porter carried my bag along a brick pathway flanked with blue petrea shrubs. It was three o'clock in the afternoon and there was one vital phone call I had to make before the end of the working day.

Inside the ground-floor room I flung my bag on the chintz-covered bed and flicked through the telephone book until I found the number I wanted. Richmond Hill Prison. I picked up the receiver and put it down again. It would be better to think through exactly what I was going to say. But I could not take too long or the administration office would shut for the day and the staff leave for home. Twice more I picked up the phone and replaced it. If the Commissioner was not there, well that would be fate. I would leave the next day.

It was even possible that the prisoner would not remember me after all this time. Why had I come back? No-one had ever pieced together exactly what happened in those days of bloodshed and confusion. Would I be able to find out anything more? Probably not. The victims of the first massacre were never found. It was rumoured that the Americans had spirited the bodies away rather than let a shrine build up around a known burial place. Certainly the truth never came out in the trial. The name of the prisoner I wanted to visit was Alleyne Devon. I had not been in touch with him since he was sentenced, originally to death, later to life in prison.

The air-conditioning made me shiver. I opened the doors onto the beach to let in some warm air. A huge mahogany tree shaded my room. I fumbled with the handset again for a few seconds then dialled the number. I was put through to the Commissioner.

'Oh, good afternoon.' I made my voice sound as polite and deferential as possible. 'I've just arrived on the island. I'm leaving again tomorrow afternoon and I wondered if there was any possibility of my visiting Mr Alleyne Devon. I was a friend of his many years ago. I do apologise for asking you at such short notice . . . I just thought I would take the opportunity while I was here.'

His voice was only a little wary. 'I think that should be all right. What is your name?'

'Eva Maybank.'

'Please be here at eleven o'clock in the morning. I will leave your name at the gate and I will inform Mr Devon.'

It was that easy. No security check. No forms needed. No fuss.

That evening I went out to the beach just before sunset. The sands were still hot underfoot. I walked along the silver scalloped outline of the incoming tide. On one side of the harbour, a huge square-fronted American cruise liner rested at anchor. It seemed huge compared with the clusters of tiny houses on land. Light from the setting sun made its whiteness spectrally brilliant. I remembered the American president's TV broadcast around the time of their invasion. He addressed the world in close-up like a monstrous uncle, speaking in a paternalistic tone:

'And we thought that it was just a pretty little tourist island, but no it wasn't. We were wrong. It was a hot-bed of communists and spies. And the Cubans were not building an airport. No sir. No sirree. They were constructing a missile base which could have threatened the shores of America. That's why we invaded. And we needed to rescue some of our American students from there too.'

There was no missile base. The half-built civilian airport was manned by local workers and the Cuban workers who had come to help.

Suddenly I was made fearful by footsteps at my back. I looked round. A honey-coloured cow with white muzzle and sad black eyes was plodding along behind me towards the sea-grape bushes.

Of course, there was always the possibility that Alleyne might refuse the visit. When I had first arrived on the island to take up a teaching post, I had stayed with him and his wife Zenia for two days before I moved to a guest house. In fact, I met Zenia first. She came to greet me at the airport, a tall smiling woman with a baby of about eighteen months slung across her hip, a welcoming warmth spilling from her as we walked to the waiting vehicle.

147

'What a lovely child.' I nodded towards the baby girl straddled on her hip.

'Yes. Mummy's only baby. Mummy's only darling.' She lifted the baby right up in the air where she kicked as if swimming in the blue sky. I remarked on how enthusiastic and friendly everyone seemed. Her proud smile held a touch of surprise.

'Of course. We're full of revolutionary spirit.'

My most vivid memory of Alleyne Devon was when he came to the guest house one evening a short while after I had moved there. Two agronomists from Tanzania were also staying there and he wanted to talk to them. We sat with the Africans out on the verandah. Alleyne was twenty-six years old and a major in the People's Revolutionary Army. He looked handsome in his officer's uniform, black trousers with a red stripe and a khaki shirt. The evening sun touched his ebony cheeks with gold. His spotless military jacket hung over the back of his chair. Even in conversation there was a tremendous sense of purpose about him. He rocked his chair back and put his feet on the rail. One of the Africans, a small man with a twisted face, was talking about the necessity of discipline in any party that came to power after a successful revolution. Alleyne listened intently then wagged his finger.

'We must learn from you people. That's why it's so good that socialists come from other countries to visit us. I agree with you about party discipline but perhaps that is because I am in the army. You have to train yourself to do things you don't want to do for the sake of others.' He leaned forward and spoke with enthusiasm: 'I do believe that if you want to serve the people in the best possible way you must submit yourself and your own needs to the requirements of your political party. You must give yourself up to the greater good. It's your duty as a revolutionary.'

He leaned back again in his chair and lapsed into silence. The guest house was situated on a steep hillside and the scene he beheld was one of poverty, a narrow ravine with clumps of rock, speckled with poor wooden shacks and tiny allotments. I remember his gaze as he looked out over the gorge. It was as though all his hopes were fixed on some distant citadel that he and he alone could see on the far side of the valley.

Later that evening a military vehicle drew up in front of the guest house and to my astonishment the prime minister himself jumped out. I am always surprised at the informality of Caribbean leaders who turn up unannounced and mix easily with the populace, happy to be addressed by their first name. He was plump, bearded and wore an unbuttoned khaki shirt-jack and jeans. He greeted us all with carefree geniality. Then he shook hands with the Africans and thanked them for coming. Everywhere there was a spirit of camaraderie and optimism. Islanders were even up early and out jogging in the mornings. The prime minister left after a while and the rest of us stayed up talking politics way into the night.

Since then I have tried to recall anything that would help me to understand how Alleyne, my friend, might have been involved in the murder of that popular, much-loved prime minister, unless it was because he considered it in some way to be his duty . . . unless the clue lay in that imaginary citadel . . . unless he believed that the distant gleaming citadel demanded those bloody sacrifices.

*

In fact, not everyone proved to be so friendly. My first literacy class took place upstairs in a wooden schoolroom bare of everything but chairs. One unshaded electric light bulb hung from the centre of the ceiling. About thirty adults attended. A small, anxious-to-please man called Jarvis had been appointed to help me. One of his cheeks sported a huge carbuncle.

'I am a policeman,' he informed me. 'A revolutionary police-man,' he added proudly while re-arranging the cheap metal chairs into a semi-circle facing me. The students were mainly poor farmers, gaunt, toothless and badly dressed, and house-wives, some massively overweight and some scrawny. They wandered in and took their places, looking askance at each other and avoiding my eyes.

As I was about to start the class, a heavily-set young woman with her hair in corn-row plaits stalked in, took a chair, turned it round and banged it down deliberately with her back to me. Disregarding her I began the class by introducing myself. Then I asked everyone to tell me their name. Some mumbled. Some spoke clearly but the young woman with her back to me stared morosely out of the window and refused to speak. I continued teaching. The policeman began to show signs of agitation. He cast anxious glances first at the young woman and then at me. He began to make clucking sounds and shake his head. Eventually, he got up and addressed her.

'This won't do, Cyrene. Have some manners, please,' he began to plead. 'We have a guest here. A visitor. What will she think of our community? What will she think of our revolution?'

The young woman did not budge. She sat there, an immove-able rock.

'Wha' she doin?' whispered one of the students.

'Me na know. She jus' deh,' replied her neighbour.

150

This was not good enough for the policeman, who felt personally responsible for the success of the class, good international relations and possibly the success of the entire revolution. He muttered and cast disappointed glances at the immobile hulk who by now had become the focus of the whole class. When I finished teaching he jumped to his feet and made an effusive speech of thanks. Then he attempted to make amends.

'To make up for the rudeness of one of our community, I am now going to sing a song.'

He gave a coy smile and began to sing 'Michael Row the Boat Ashore, Hallelujah'. In the middle of the song, the sulker rose to her feet and stomped out of the room. The singing policeman finished his tuneful performance with regret shining in his eyes.

The next day a small bomb went off at precisely 7pm under a podium in a school hall where the prime minister was due to speak. The prime minister was saved by the Caribbean habit of arriving late for events. No-one was injured but the floorboards by the podium were badly damaged. It was commonly accepted that American CIA agents had planted the bomb. Anxious rumours started to sweep the island. Out at sea the United States navy was conducting a manoeuvre involving a mock attack on a small socialist island. Alleyne, who was part of the government's Central Committee, took me and some other comrades to inspect the damage. He looked distressed as he pushed away the damaged boards with his foot:

'Ordinary people could have been hurt here. We are not used to this sort of thing on our island. We must be vigilant.'

He took off his scarlet cap with its black laminated peak and passed a worried hand over his forehead as he spoke:

'It is important that we keep our revolution safe.'

I continued with my work which took me all over the island. I travelled in the baking heat to rural communities and taught literacy classes in wooden halls, zinc-roofed sheds and sometimes on scorching ground in the open air.

Back in the capital rifts had begun to occur in the government. There had been a schism. The deputy prime minister had suggested joint leadership with the prime minister. He was suspicious of the prime minister's easy-going manner and enormous popularity. He believed it bordered on a personality cult. His burly figure could often be seen walking in front of the prime minister to remind everyone that the people's revolutionary government was a collective enterprise. He thought that the political structures of the revolution should be cast in iron and had unshakeable confidence in the rigour of his political analysis. The prime minister had a different approach. He was relaxed and joked with people. He turned up late for meetings. His girlfriend was pregnant. There were rumours of other women. He delayed attending a military parade because he was visiting a friend in hospital. The opposition cabal who supported the deputy prime minister held special meetings to censure the prime minister for lack of discipline. Alleyne Devon was one of them. In the background was the threat of the United States and its naval manoeuvres. Before anyone knew quite how or why, the prime minister, the most popular politician in the country, had been put under house arrest by the opposing faction.

I returned to the capital a short while later. The place was in turmoil. I was in my small apartment near Fort Rupert when I heard Alleyne making an announcement on the radio:

'It must be clearly understood that the People's Revolutionary

Army and the Armed Forces as a whole will tolerate absolutely no manifestation whatsoever of counter-revolution.'

The next day I left my apartment to buy plantain from the market. There was a hubbub in the street and I turned a corner to find myself confronted by an enormous crowd of excited people who had managed to release their much-loved prime minister. There was a general sense of jubilation. I caught a glimpse of his smiling bearded face as he was swept along by the crowd. Microphones had already been set up for him to speak at Market Square. Then there was a sudden change of plan and he and the clamorous crowd turned and headed for the army headquarters at Fort Rupert. Everyone seemed good-humoured but determined. In the throng I spotted my friend Maeva bouncing along in her lime-green shorts and yellow t-shirt:

'We gat 'im free. Freedom!' she yelled at me in triumph, flinging her arms in the air and waving them about.

I went back home intending to come out later and see what was happening.

It must have been just about then that Alleyne Devon and other army officers, who were in another barracks, heard of the prime minister's release. It was said that Alleyne shouted angrily to his troops that the newly freed prime minister had betrayed the masses. Two armoured vehicles and a truck were dispatched with instructions to recover possession of the army headquarters at Fort Rupert which had been taken over by the crowd.

From my flat I could hear 'Pop pop popopopopop'. Gunfire. Then, about ten minutes later, more shots. Popop. Pop pop popopopop. I thought people were firing off rifles to celebrate the prime minister's release. Fifteen minutes later there was a frantic banging on my front door. It was Maeva, the friend whom I had just left in the crowd:

'Murder!' she was shouting. 'Murder. Quick. Quick. Eva. Help. Open the door.'

I opened the door reluctantly. She was panting. Her lime-green shorts had been torn when she scaled a railing.

'Dem a dead.'

The news had ricocheted through the crowd. People scattered in panic. The prime minister, who minutes before had been laughing with the crowd of liberators, along with his pregnant girlfriend, two trade union leaders and three other supporters, lay slaughtered in the stone compound which ran with blood. The killings lasted no more than three minutes. Massacres do not always take long.

A few days after the massacre the Americans invaded in Operation Urgent Fury. Alleyne and other members of the Central Committee were detained in metal containers from the docks. The seismic shock of the American invasion concussed the island. A friend hurried to my apartment and warned me to leave.

'Get out while you can. The Americans are arresting people who supported the government. They've killed some of the Cubans who put up a resistance.'

At the airport I sat with other would-be passengers on the dried brown grass outside. Five heavily armed American soldiers trained guns on us. After a while an American jeep drove up. Two U.S. army majors got out with three islanders. They walked among us trying to identify anyone connected to the revolutionary government. Five men were manhandled into the jeep. The rest of us were allowed to board the plane.

*

This was my first return to the island since then. In the morning I called a taxi.

'Richmond Hill prison, please.'

The taxi driver looked at me with dislike. He had guessed immediately that I was going to visit one of the long-term political prisoners. Even after all this time they were hated. A few minutes after we left the hotel he swerved and took an unnecessary detour so that we passed Fort Rupert.

'That's where our Prime Minister was executed.' His face burned with rage. 'Dey shoulda hang dem people.'

The taxi began the long zig-zagging ride up the steep mountain slowing down at hairpin bends. Morne Jaloux. The sad road sign looked down at us from a bend in the road. Below I could see the harbour and the huge American luxury liner now heading towards the horizon slowly like a dream.

A guard stopped us at the prison's main entrance which consisted of nothing more than a tubular metal framed gate criss-crossed with chicken wire.

'I have an appointment with the Commissioner.'

I was too nervous to use Alleyne's name in the face of the taxi driver's fury.

The guard nodded and allowed the gate to swing open. I was dropped off outside a single-storey office. I stated my business and the woman behind the desk asked me to wait outside. I sat on a bench in the brilliant sunshine.

After I had left the island twenty-five years earlier, I tried to follow the chaotic trial from abroad. The tribunal was funded by the United States. One witness testified that Alleyne had been in Fort Frederick barracks when the prime minister was freed; that he had accused the prime minister of spreading vicious rumours against the Central Committee and said that the prime minister was supported by counter-revolutionaries in league with American big business. He had persuaded the soldiers that these elements must be liquidated to preserve the revolution and save the people of the island. The witness said that Alleyne then shouted 'Long Live the Central Committee. Long live the revolution. The Central Committee orders.' And the soldiers shouted back 'We obey. We obey.'

A second witness denied all this saying that the first witness was already under arrest at the time and seated on a tea-chest and had not been in a position to see or hear any such goings on. This second witness stated that everyone was in a state of total paralysis because the Central Committee was demoralised and ineffective.

There followed weeks of contradictory and confused testimonies.

Then came the death sentences. I heard that Alleyne was on death row alongside thirteen of the others waiting to be hanged within a day or so. I tried to telephone Zenia. The phone was disconnected. The gallows were ready and two other executioners had been brought in from outside the island because of the numbers involved. Then I heard that the sentences had been commuted to life imprisonment. Alleyne had been in jail for the last twenty-five years.

A guard was tapping me on the shoulder and pointing towards the doors of the prison visiting room up a narrow lane. That morning there were only two visitors. There was a poorly dressed, haggard woman who walked haltingly up the incline carrying two water coconuts for her son. I followed her.

The visiting room was large, concrete and airy with a wooden ceiling that sloped down on either side from a main beam like the upturned hull of a great boat. Two relaxed prison officers were re-arranging the long tables like school desks and placing benches on either side of them. When they had finished we were called over to have our names written down in a book. The woman offered up her two green water coconuts for inspection and I showed them a book I had brought for Alleyne. Realising at the last moment that I should bring something and not really knowing what he might like, I had bought a copy of Conrad's *Lord Jim* at the airport, forgetting that it was about a man who in haste makes a disastrous decision.

Two men entered from the other side of the hall wearing dark blue denim prison garb. For a moment I was confused. Alleyne Devon had been a young man when I last saw him and so for a minute I looked over at the younger man. But I gradually recognised Alleyne in the middle-aged man who was looking in my direction. His closely cropped hair was now white and his features heavier and lined. But it was him.

We acknowledged each other cautiously and sat down on opposite sides of a table whose polished top was etched and scored with age.

'Hello Alleyne. I wasn't sure that you would remember me. Do you?'

He ran his hand over his forehead. It was a gesture I remembered.

'I think so. No. I'm sorry. I'm not sure that I do.'

I reminded him of my brief stay at his house; how we had inspected the bomb damage together; the long wrangling political debates at night; the prime minister's visit to the guest house. At the mention of the prime minister his face closed.

'Something is beginning to come back. It was all such a long time ago. But I do now remember you.'

We talked about what he had been doing. He filled in some of the gaps.

'You know, I have been studying divinity. I have a B.A. external degree from London University. I was a staunch Methodist as a youngster. I have gone back to my religious roots.'

It made sense somehow, the youthful religious fervour turning into revolutionary political zeal. As he talked, I recognised that the man I had known was still a man who desired to transform the world. The revolution that was his ideal had been so perfect, so blazingly pure and inviolable and such a salvation for the poorest people of his island that he was willing to do anything to sustain it. Even, as seemed to be the case, murder.

'I still have my political beliefs,' he said in a low voice. 'I have not lost those. But I am an ordained minister now. I work with the drug-addicted and the disadvantaged in here. I encountered God in this prison. My salvation. I've sung my Redemption Song, the song of atonement. I try to help people.'

The guards talked quietly in a corner of the room. He went on:

'I have learnt so much in this place. I am almost grateful for the opportunity to have learned so much. But when I get out, I won't be able to stay on the island.' There was regret in his voice. He knew the islanders hated him. There had been threats of lynching. 'Perhaps I can go to Africa.'

There was a familiar gleam in his eye, a yearning to use what was left of his life to make a difference somewhere. It was the old fervour, banked down, waiting to re-ignite.

A block on my tongue made me unable to ask the question 'Did you order the killings?'

As if my thoughts were written on my face, he looked directly at me and said: 'I owe a debt to humanity.'

Was that a confession? The sunlight caught the whitened hair at his temples.

One of the guards came over and tapped his watch showing that it was time for the visit to finish. Alleyne asked me for a pen.

'Please get in touch with Zenia. I'm sure she'd like to hear from you.'

He scribbled her telephone number on the piece of paper I handed him.

'I'll try. I'm leaving this afternoon.'

He stood up. There was a sort of buoyancy about him now as if he were full of air and might be able to fly to Africa like Macandal. The visit had refreshed him. He looked like a plant after light rain, ready to put out fresh shoots and buds. We shook hands across the table. He said goodbye and walked out of the visiting room studying the copy of Lord Jim I had given him. He did not look back.

On the way back down the hill the thump of reggae music echoed across the valley. The small wooden dwellings perched on the hillsides looked unkempt and dejected, lost and disillusioned. It felt like a murdered island.

Back at the hotel I just had time to telephone Zenia before heading for the airport. She remembered me straight away and asked:

'How did you manage to get a visit?'

'I just telephoned yesterday and asked to speak to the Commissioner.'

She sucked her teeth:

'You were lucky. It's not always so easy. People are often refused. It's quite arbitrary. Sometimes the authorities are terrible.'

She came to the airport and we talked a little about her life and her daughter who was now sitting her exams at college. The result of another appeal was due any day.

'If Alleyne is released we plan to go to Mali and start a new life there. We can't stay here. You know he is an ordained minister now. They have several Methodist missionary outposts in Mali. Alleyne is learning to speak French.' She sat with her hands in her lap, both resigned and hopeful.

And then I said out of the blue: 'I always remember you saying you were full of revolutionary spirit. We all were. What happened?

There was a long pause before Zenia answered, 'I don't know. It was an epidemic.'

She waved goodbye as I went through the departures gate. An hour and twenty minutes later my plane was rising through the air leaving the island behind me.

I telephoned her again to congratulate them when I heard that the appeal had been successful.

About four years later an article in the newspaper caught my attention. A Methodist mission in Mali, somewhere north of the River Niger, had been under threat from a small group of Islamic militants. In a pre-emptive attempt to safeguard his Christian mission and thwart any attack, the minister had shot the militants dead. The minister had since disappeared and was thought to be somewhere in the bush outside Timbuktu.

A BRIGHT YELLOW BAG

Gina Fiore thanked the assistant who ushered her into the brightly lit clinical side room on the second floor of Edinburgh's Royal Infirmary. The window faced on to a brick wall. Next to the examination bed stood a gleaming instrument trolley behind which was a small sink. There was a chair available but it seemed somehow wrong to sit down.

After a few minutes a white-coated junior doctor let himself into the room and shook her hand. His first impression was of a thin anxious girl in her twenties with a slightly crooked smile, her blonde hair twisted into a top-knot. There was an awkward pause before the doctor spoke.

'We do apologize for everything that's happened. There are some X-rays here if you would like to see them. They were part of the research. I take it you speak English?'

'Yes. Thank you.' She was not sure she wanted to see the X-rays.

The doctor slotted an X-ray plate into the cabinet hanging on the wall and flicked the light switch.

Set against the cosmic blackness of the X-ray plate, the exposed brain resembled the trans-section of a halved white cauliflower, the stalk rising through the centre and branching off into florets. The doctor pointed out a patch of what looked like dark filmy webbing:

'The patch that intrudes into the brain here is behind the occipital lobe near the reticular formation. That is where an operation was performed. We think that took place several years before your mother was . . .'

'In prison.' She finished the sentence for him and twisted her blue silk scarf around the straps of her handbag.

'Yes.'

'It was an operation to remove a tumour, wasn't it? That's what I was told.'

'No. It wasn't a tumour. It was an aneurism. Look. Here is the tiny capillary clamp.'

This was confusing. She had always been told that her mother had suffered a brain tumour. The prison authorities wanted to perform a second operation. Her mother, who had been convicted of various bombings and an attempted kidnap, did not trust the authorities and had refused permission. She was found hanging in her cell shortly afterwards. Her fellow activists remained convinced that she had been murdered by the Italian state. It was a time of political upheaval, of wild rumour and suspicion. The authorities maintained it was suicide.

After the court case and the death, Gina's father had fled from Milan to Padova with his young daughter. There he lived in an apartment on the Via Orsovo working as a teaching assistant and raising his shy wispy child as best he could. When she was little he told her that her mother was with the angels. When she was older he told her that her mother had been on the side of the angels. Occasionally Gina sneaked a look in the bureau drawer at the black and white press clippings which showed her mother looking grim and intense and not like an angel at all. When she was seventeen her father died and Gina found work with a local estate agent, enjoying the routine and security of office life. Like many children of radicals, Gina showed no interest in politics.

Then one day while she was sitting in the kitchen eating breakfast, a letter from Edinburgh arrived.

In a revelation embarrassing to both the British and Italian authorities it disclosed that, after her death in the San Vittore women's jail, her mother's brain had been lifted from the cranium without authorization. The brain had been sent to Edinburgh University for a joint research project. The professor of neuropathology in charge of the original research had been looking for 'terrorist' pathology but after several years had found nothing. When he retired, a psychiatrist and another doctor had undertaken some further research, comparing the brain with those of serial killers. Nothing significant was found there either. The research had been put to one side and then forgotten. However, after a scandal and public outcry in England where a hospital had kept body parts without permission, various institutions looked into their laboratory archives and Gina's mother's remains came to light. Once the ethical committee of the university had taken the decision to return the brain a letter of apology had been sent to the Fiore family. It included a request for the remains to be collected.

Gina took leave from work without explaining why. She arrived in Edinburgh, where the brain remained in a jar of formaldehyde, with only a vague idea of what to do with it, but she thought she should have it interred with the rest of her mother's remains in Italy.

'Do I need to sign anything?' she enquired.

'Er . . . I don't think so. I haven't got anything for you to sign anyway.'

The doctor stood on a chair and took the brain from the top shelf of a cupboard. The jar was a large standard preserving jar. He handed it over. Gina took hold of it carefully with both hands. The grey mass floated in the moving liquid.

'Do you want the X-rays?

'No thank you.'

'Do you need a carrier bag or anything?' He asked. 'I'll see if I can find one of our lab assistants.'

She sat there looking out of the window at the brick wall outside, while he went to fetch someone. After about eight minutes he re-appeared with a toothy lad in green overalls carrying a large bright yellow industrial plastic bag.

'This is Dave. You can put the jar in that bag. Dave will show you the way out.'

'Thank you very much.' Gina placed the jar carefully in the bag. She gathered up her things, then put the bright yellow bag over her arm.

Outside the main entrance Gina stood at the top of the stone steps feeling a little sick. A cold March wind blew strands of hair across her face.

'De ye want me tae chum ye tae the bus stop?' The lad asked, then seeing her puzzled expression he re-phrased the question:

'Wull ah go with ye tae show ye the way?'

'Oh, please. Thank you.'

Dave chatted as he strode along:

'It's ma job tae clean oot the rats in the lab at the university. They keep the rats in an area wi an electrified grid all roon it.

It's ma job tae keep the rats comfortable. I gie them plenty of food an they huv plenty of space. But every time they try tae leave the area they get an electric shock frae the grid. Onyway, they soon learn no tae touch the grid an tae live in comfort. But efter a while they get bored, eh, an they tak the risk. In the end they'll risk treadin on the grid an gettin an electric shock jist tae get oot intae the unknown an explore an huv a bit of excitement.'

Gina was hardly listening. She was worried that the brain would be damaged by bumping against the side of the glass jar as they walked.

'I widnae leave a that comfort. Ah've been in and oot o children's hames an in care. Them rats dinna ken when they're lucky.'

By now Gina was feeling distinctly unwell. Her cheeks became hot and then cold and an unpleasant overproduction of saliva filled her mouth. She stopped and stood still for a moment. Dave was looking at her. A vertiginous giddiness swirled up from the back of her head. She handed Dave the carrier bag just in time before her legs bent slowly and folded beneath her.

Dave caught her and helped her sit down on the grass verge.

'Phew. Ye nearly whited. Are ye aw'right?'

Gina turned her head away and vomited into the grass. Tears came into her eyes.

'Will ah get ye a drink?'

She nodded. He put the carrier bag down beside her and ran down the road, arms and legs flailing like a windmill. A short while later he re-appeared carrying a can of Irn Bru:

'Hey,' he said suddenly. 'I dinnae even ken whaur it is you're supposed tae be gawin.'

'I've got to find a place. I came straight from the airport to the hospital before I found a hotel. I was going to take a bus to the centre of town and find somewhere.'

Dave sat on the ground and waited for her to recover. He snapped his fingers.

'Ah'll tell ye whit. I'll tak ye tae ma pal Jimmy's place. It's only doon the road and ye cud lie doon there fur a wee bitty. Ma pal Jimmy, his ma has just died. His brother's a bit o' a smack-heid but they're ok. Ye can find a wee hotel when ye feel better.'

She nodded. When she felt strong enough they walked on. It was half past ten in the morning. Rows of clammy grey stone houses broke out in a tubercular sweat as the early morning frost melted.

Dave pushed open the front door of a tall tenement building. A damp chill from the stone stairwell engulfed them. Gina stepped back as four youths clutching cans of Stella Artois came clattering down the stairs. The one in front executed a strange dance step, then when he saw Dave and Gina he put his finger to his lips, pointed to the front door of the ground floor flat to their left and mouthed, 'Psycho.'

From under the front door of the ground floor flat came the smell of grass being smoked and the sound of country and western music.

'Psycho's in,' explained Dave to Gina. 'Psycho's a bit wrang in the heid. He disnae work. He's only slim but he's got this enormous swagger on him.'

The four boys were creeping past Psycho's flat.

Suddenly Psycho's front door opened. A short man with a scar the size of a ravine running from the side of his mouth stood in the doorway:

'Mmmn. Four drunkie boys.' He rubbed his hands together as he saw the four youths. The boys fell over each other trying to get away from him. Psycho followed them into the street. When they were at a safe distance one of them turned back, kicked an empty can of Stella at him and shouted:

'Haw. Have ye got a licence for that swagger?'

Psycho stood in the street staring after the boys.

As he led Gina up the stairs Dave explained. 'Sometimes Psycho gets ye by the scruff of the neck then he pushes your head doon so your nose is nearly touchin the pavement an maks ye recite all the names of the Rangers fitba' team. If ye get wan wrong ye get battered.'

In the front room of the first floor flat two dark haired lads sat on the floor in front of a black plastic settee whose torn surface spilled stuffing. Their heads wagged with mischievous sagacity in time to ear-splitting hard house music. The only colour in the room came from the television which blazed like a bunch of flowers in the corner. One of the lads held up a bandaged thumb in greeting.

Dave shouted over the music: 'This is Gina. She needs somewhere tae lie doon. Whaur's Jimmy?'

The bandaged thumb pointed to a pair of bare legs sticking out of an armchair opposite the television.

Dave glanced over. 'Mornin telly's shite. Whit happent tae your thumb?'

'Three stitches. Ah smashed it through a windae efter ma step-dad wis giein us grief, eh.'

Gina felt hot and light-headed. She stood in the doorway cradling the yellow plastic bag in her arms. The room reeked of stale beer and there was ash in the crevices of the cheap patterned carpet. A black plastic bag containing jigsaws and old children's games had spilled some of its contents near the door. Dave trod through the debris of empty beer cans and torn cigarette packets and went over to the figure asleep in the chair. He tried to shake it awake.

'Haw, Jimmy.' He turned to Gina. 'He's been sleepin a lot since his maw died.'

Jimmy woke up. The face that peered tentatively around the back of the chair had wide spavined cheekbones and deep-set hazel eyes. His near transparent complexion was tinged with the blue pallor of skimmed milk. His teeth were discoloured and pearly grey. He rubbed his eyes with the back of his fists and looked around blearily.

Jimmy's mother had died on a freezing night some ten weeks previously, a few days before his sixteenth birthday. She was thirty-nine years old and had suffered a deep vein thrombosis. Her boyfriend had found her dead on the sofa in the morning. Jimmy had no jacket for the funeral. He wore a clean white shirt and a blue knotted tie and wept throughout. The night of the funeral his mother's boyfriend cleared out for good, leaving him and his seventeen-year-old brother on their own. The flat with no adults in it had become a magnet for the boys' pals.

'But ah still see him,' Jimmy told them. 'He gies us money for bread an milk an at. Ma real dad turned up fur the funeral. When he saw I hud nae jaiket he came roond an brought me this jaiket. Then he starts greetin and wailin. He was steamin, eh.' Jimmy mimicked him: 'Oh ma son. Ma son. Here ye are, ma son. Here's somethin fur ye.' He gied me this jaiket an a block of cheese frae the kitchens in the hospital whaur he works then he niver came back. So I've hud lots of cheese on toast and macaroni cheese since ma maw died.'

'Jimmy. There's a girl here. She's sick, eh. She's Italian. Can she lie doon here fur a wee while, eh?'

Jimmy got to his feet, stretched slowly and yawned. A creased shirt hung halfway down his bare thighs. His shoulder blades protruded like angular wings. He had slept the night where he lay in the chair.

'Wha?'

Just then there was a loud regular thumping sound from the flat above. Jimmy yawned again and picked up the broom leaning against the television. He thumped the ceiling several times with the long handle. Then he explained.

'When we play oor music too loud the people upstairs they bang down at us and we bang up at them.'

One of the boys on the sofa started to yell up at the ceiling in time to the music:

'Oi oi you nutters. Oi oi you nutters.'

'Fucking shut up a minute, ye cunt,' Jimmy complained. He turned to Dave. 'Whit's that ye're sayin?'

'She nearly passed oot. She needs tae lie down. Could she no have your mam's bed?'

'Nah.' Jimmy looked anguished. 'That's ma mam's room. I havenae touched it since she died.' He turned to Gina. 'Mam kept her bedroom door locked because we used tae steal things. Noo I wish we hadnae. Wid ye be wantin a cup of tea or sumthin?'

Gina shook her head. She slid weakly down the door jamb and sat on the floor. The hairclip fastening her hair came undone and her blonde hair fell loose around her shoulders as she put her head in her hands. This had an effect on the boys. They all stared at her. The two sitting on the sofa stood up to leave as if something untoward had happened which required their departure before they were held responsible for anything.

'Ok. See youse a later,' they said as they edged past Gina and out through the door.

Dave followed them and they all disappeared down the stairs. Jimmy was left on his own looking sullen and annoyed.

'I suppose I could let you intae ma mam's room. But don't touch anythin.' He found the key to the room and opened it. Gina went in first.

The musty sadness of the room enveloped her. A double bed with a cheap veneer headboard took up most of the space. It was covered by a pink candlewick bedspread. An old wardrobe was crammed in next to the door. On the bedside table was a heart-shaped photograph frame with a picture of Jimmy and his elder brother Brian. Jimmy spotted his mother's teeth in a glass by the bed:

'That's ma mam's teeth there. The hospital gied us them back.' He stared at them. Gina looked down at her yellow carrier bag and remained silent.

'Ah'll just leave you, then. The bathroom's doon the corridor at the end.'

As soon as Jimmy shut the door behind him Gina stowed the yellow bag under the bed, lay down and fell into an exhausted asleep. She woke at three in the morning knowing she was going to be violently sick. Feeling her way down the narrow hall to the bathroom she passed the open door of the front room. By the light of the TV she could see Jimmy's figure hanging half upside down off the edge of the sofa, one leg thrown over the back.

When she had finished being sick in the bathroom she made her way to the kitchen. Someone had stubbed a cigarette out in a jar of marmalade. She found a tea-stained mug and took some water back to the bedroom.

In the numb grey light of morning she was awoken by fierce incomprehensible whispers outside her door.

'Ah telt ye no tae bring that stuff in here. I promised mam ah wouldnae touch it.'

'Ye don't huv tae fuckin touch it. Ah wis blootered with it last night though. Who is this lassie anyway?'

'Ah dunno. Italian or summat. She's sleepin.'

'Ask her if she's got ony money.'

'You ask.'

'Did you lift up her skirt and have a look.'

'Naw. At least Ah've got some morals.'

'Huv ye fuck ye wee cunt. Yir jist a poof.'

Jimmy took a swing and landed a crashing punch on his brother's chin. A minute later the flat was resounding to vicious thumps and bangs and hoarse yells:

'Get oot of ma fuckin room. Get oot. You jist comes into ma room and tak things.'

'Let me borrow them jeans.'

'No.'

'Ya selfish wee bastard. Yir no wearin them.'

'Fuck off.'

A door slammed. Gina could hear someone singing to the rap music that suddenly roared through the flat: *Fuck you too motherfucker.*

The music hammered through the air making the walls vibrate and worsening her headache.

Jimmy poked his head around the door. A bluish trans-parency about him reminded her of an embryonic baby bird

171

fallen prematurely from the nest. She lifted her head from the bed.

'I'm sorry. I am still sick. I have a bad flu I think.'

'D'ye want a cup of tea or anythin? Ah heard ye spewin up in the night.' Jimmy grunted. 'We wis fightin. It's ma brother's fault. We got a warnin frae the council. They sent a man roon tae see us.'

She raised herself on one elbow :

'I think I am all right. If I can just lie here until I feel better. Then I'll look for a hotel.'

Jimmy was unsure of what to do. It felt odd seeing this blonde creature in his mother's bed. When she spoke. he reared gently away avoiding eye contact but with a faint smile of pleasure on his lips:

'Ah can get ye a bite tae eat. There's no much here but what I dae is I get a heel of bread an ah toast one side. Then ah put Dolmio sauce on it and a bit of cheese an it's like a pizza.'

Gina felt immediately ill. 'Not just yet, thank you.' She smiled again. 'Just because I am Italian doesn't mean I like pizza.'

'Whit's bein Italian got tae dae with pizza?' he asked. This time he looked at her directly and then looked away again 'If ye hear us rowin dinnae worry. Ma brother Brian is back. Ah fuckin' hate the bastard. But he's all I've got. We've only got each other now.' He left shutting the door behind him.

After a few minutes Gina pushed back the thin coverlet and got up. She bent down and pulled the yellow plastic bag and its contents from under the bed. Then she opened the wardrobe door and placed the bag in the bottom of the wardrobe under the few dresses that hung there. She went back to bed. A few minutes later she took the yellow bag out of the wardrobe again and put it back under the bed.

It was ten past eleven in the morning when Gina emerged. She went into the front room to find Brian. He had a thin, vicious face and an Adam's apple that bobbed up and down as he talked on his mobile. He was sitting on the sofa naked but for an old green towel tied round his waist. With his other hand he scratched under his arms. When he saw Gina he threw out his slat-ribbed chest, stretched his arms in the air and waved hello before switching his phone off.

'Hiya. Ah'm Brian. Jimmy's away doon the road at our gran's.'

She was bending forward slightly because of pains in her stomach.

'If I gave you some money do you think someone could get me aspirin or something from a chemist for flu?'

'Nae bother.'

'How much money would you need?'

'Jist gie us a sky-diver. A fiver. Huv ye got euros? Can ah hae a look at wan?'

She showed him a euro which he examined with curiosity then she handed him a twenty-pound note.

'Aw. Magic.' He grabbed the money. She waited in the kitchen. Twenty minutes later Brian burst back into the flat and began stacking an old box freezer with chips, pizzas and chicken nuggets:

'Weh-hey. The breakfast fairy's been. Yiv nae idea how good that makes me feel.' He rubbed his hands together with pleasure and spun on his heel. The front door slammed behind him and he was gone. In the ensuing peace she found the jar of aspirins and a packet of Lemsip.

Jimmy let himself back into the flat. He was out of breath as he manhandled a hoover into the front room. He came into the kitchen where Gina waited for a kettle to boil. He looked at her directly as he spoke, relating his story in a matter-of-fact monotone which had the detached realism of the messenger in a Greek tragedy:

'I just went tae borrow this Dyson from ma gran. I have tae carry the hoover back and forward 'cos oors is bust. She's been greetin ever since ma maw died. They wasnae jist mother and daughter. They wis best pals. They did everything together. They went tae Weight-Watchers together. But when ah got there just noo she'd fell and hit her eye in the bathroom. She wis steamin. She'd drunk a bottle o whisky an a bottle of vodka. Her eye wis a black. I said "Yir gaun tae your bed" an I tried tae put her tae bed but she struggled and then she was hangin oot of the bed and I thought she'd fall. I pushed her to the far side of the bed but she grabbed another bottle and started drinkin that.' Jimmy's face was white with distress. 'She wus cryin and ah didnae know whit tae dae so ah just gied her a cuddle.'

He had tried to put his grandmother to bed but she wept inconsolably. In the end he gave up. He had left the tenement block to the sound of her shrieking and wailing as she dragged herself up the stairs banging dolefully on each of her neighbours' doors in turn.

When he finished speaking he gave Gina a nod as if to indicate that he had finished his report. Then he went back into the front room and switched on the vacuum cleaner.

*

In between bouts of sickness and sleep, Gina could detect no regular rhythm to the household in which she found herself. One moment the flat was full of noisy music and there was mysterious shouting and gleeful yells. The next moment there was the sound of running feet and the place was deserted. There were long periods when the flat was empty. Her bones ached and she could not eat. After two days of sickness she wanted to wash. There was no hot water. The shower had broken. The steady thump of a cd playing in the front room rocked the walls. She crept into the bathroom and sponged herself down with cold water from the tap. After that she boiled some water for a better wash. Up and dressed, Gina went in to where Jimmy lay on his bed in his room.

'How's your gran?' she asked Jimmy.

'She's aw right. Ah'll tak ye roon there when yir feelin better.'

'I feel a bit better now. I must leave soon and find somewhere else to stay. Then I will go back to Italy.'

'Ye can stay here if ye want till yir better.'

Since Gina's arrival Jimmy felt that a benign presence had entered the house. He made small attempts to improve things. Just now he was wearing only his jeans because he'd washed his best t-shirt and hung it on a radiator to dry. But the heating had gone off. Jimmy stole glances at her:

'Did ye see ma lamp?' He leaned over and switched on his bedside lamp. 'It changes colours. It's fibre optic. I saw it in a shop. It was only nine pound. It's nice, eh?' He watched the lamp's fluctuating colours. 'It looks like a tropical fish.'

He took some hash out of a drawer in the bedside table:

'Wud ye like a wee bit of a doobie? Ah can mak us a joint.'

They sat on the bed passing the loosely made joint and the ashtray between them.

'I won't smoke too much,' she said. 'My head is still dizzy.'

'Ye could stay on here. Save ye the money on a hotel.' He looked at her, a hopeful query in his eyes:

'Ur ye here on holiday?'

'No.' Gina hesitated. 'I came to Scotland to do something . . . something to do with what happened to my mother when she was in jail in Italy a long time ago.'

'Oor mam was in jail too fur a wee bitty. Just a bit of shopliftin,' said Jimmy sympathetically. 'What wis yours in fur?'

Gina pushed her fair hair back from her face. The words came out in a sort of gasp: 'Murder. Kidnapping and causing explosions.'

Jimmy recoiled. An involuntary look of distaste passed over his face.

'My mother was a revolutionary,' she explained. 'They kidnapped a Catholic cardinal once to get their comrades released.'

'Ye'd better no tell ma granny that.'

She frowned as she continued. 'I think a rich banker was kidnapped. But something went wrong and he got killed. There was an informer in their group. That's how my mother was caught.'

'Ah hate a grass.'

Gina found it difficult to justify her mother's actions in the face of his solemn attention. 'My mother wanted to help working-class people.'

Jimmy looked unconvinced. 'It's still murder though.' He sounded oddly conservative. Some sense of morality had been stirred up from the bottom of a long neglected reservoir. Aware that his tone might have sounded disapproving he tried to make amends. 'Ma granny has a friend called Billy Knox. What he does is basically he takes people tae this warehouse an slaughters them. As soon as ma gran mentions his name tae people they pay her back the money they owe her.'

It was Gina's turn to look doubtful. 'That's different. My mother didn't kill innocent people. They blew up banks and government buildings at night when they were empty. My grandad was a partisan.'

Gina stopped. She could see that Jimmy was not making sense of what she was saying. Gradually, he became more relaxed. The dope kicked in and he began to enjoy the floating feeling. He lay back on the bed again with his arms folded behind his head.

'My grandad was a brickie. I never met him but gran says he used tae hang a cloth oot the windae at night an if it wis frozen in the mornin he'd go back to bed. Ye cannae lay bricks when it's freezin.'

The lamp threw a revolving pattern of coloured light onto the ceiling.

'Ah like to look at they lights when I'm stoned.'

He continued with his family history, counting off the family members on his fingers.

'Ma dad is an alcoholic. Ma step-dad is an alcoholic. Ma gran's faither was an alcoholic. Ma two uncles are on heroin – well they get methadone substitute now. They go to collect their methadone three times a week. Ma uncle can drink 50 mills of methadone and still be all right. He's that used tae it.'

He turned towards her. 'Whit's your favourite film? *One Flew Over the Cuckoo's Nest* is mine.'

Gina curled up on the stained grey duvet. A warmth was spreading through her stomach that diminished the nausea of the last few days. Jimmy looked sideways at her dark eyelashes with admiration. She had rubbed her skin with rosewater cream. He breathed in the scent of it.

She began to talk faster, sounding increasingly Italian.

'I can't really remember my mother. She was an anarchist. But later it was proved that it was the fascists who were causing the explosions and blaming it on the anarchists.' She turned to Jimmy with an indignant look on her face. Jimmy started to giggle. Gina looked at him, startled, then she began to giggle too.

'This skunk is ace,' he said.

They lay flat on their backs next to each other looking at the swirling patterns of light on the ceiling.

Gina continued: 'I work for an estate agent now.'

'Can ye get free tickets to places?'

'That's a travel agent.'

They dissolved into laughter again. The laughter subsided.

'Whit's an anarchist?'

'Someone who is against the state, I think.'

'Ah don't like the polis either. Ah'm fallin asleep here.' His lids rolled shut over his eyes.

'So am I.'

His hand was warm. He took hers and braided their fingers together as they drifted into sleep. Gina glanced at the figure beside her. Jimmy turned away on his side, his shoulder blades two folded wings, his dreams iridescent on his back.

When Jimmy and Gina returned from the off-licence later that night about ten youths between the ages of fifteen and eighteen were standing around in the front room of the flat drinking vodka and Red Bull. Zombie Lover played on the cd player. Gina found the noise overpowering and disappeared to her bedroom.

The front room was a seething den of conspiracy and whispering.

'Dinnae retaliate back.'

'He's gone ballistic. Mental.'

'Turn it up.'

'Naw. Turn it doon.'

'Never mind what he says. Turn it up, cocksucker.'

The drumming and screaming of the Zombie Lover music swelled as someone turned up the volume to full pitch.

'Haw, Jimmy. Psycho's been up.'

Jimmy put the six-packs on the coffee table. A shaven-headed youth sitting on the sofa grabbed a Heineken.

'Someone left the door open and Psycho marched right in, eh. I tried tae shut the door on him but the doorknob came off in ma hand. He wis carryin a can of Lynx deodorant in wan hand and a high velocity airgun in the ither. We aw tried to find somewhere to hide, right? He just went intae the kitchen an sprayed the deodorant ontae the washing-up tub full o' water. Then he lit it. This blue flame exploded an lit up the whole kitchen. Then he came in here and shot at a your Celtic posters. See – they're a pitted wi slugs.'

Jimmy went to see the damage in the kitchen.

'Whaur's Brian?' he asked.

'He'll be back in a minute.'

Just then Brian walked in and threw down his jacket. 'Dave can ye cut us hair for us please?'

'Psycho's been in and tried to blow up your kitchen.'

Brian pulled up a chair and sat in it. He put a tea towel round his shoulders. 'I dinna gie a fuck. Ah want ma hair cut. Pronto.'

Dave took the electric clippers and began to shave Brian's head. With his head only half shaved, the electricity failed.

The music and the clippers stopped working at the same time. Brian jumped up from his seat in a panic:

'Fix it. Fix it ye cunt or Ah'll kill ye,' he yelled. 'Look at ma hair. Ah'll no be able to go oot like this.'

Everyone looked in awe at his half-shaven head. Someone went to put fifty pence in the meter. The clippers motor and the music started up again. Dave went on with the job.

'Whaur's the broom?' asked Dave, looking at all the hair on the floor.

'Whistle an it'll come tae ye, ye cunt.' Brian's good humour returned.

That seemed to be a signal for them all to pile on top of each other on the sofa in a joyous muddle like a scrum of puppies. The music pounded:

'I think Jimmy's in love with yon Italian bird.'

'No Ah'm no,' said Jimmy.

'She's knock-kneed.'

'No, she isnae.'

'Ye fancy her tho' don't ye?'

'She's aw right.'

'She's old. She must be twenty or even thirty.'

'She's not fucking thirty. Ma mum was only thirty-nine when she died.'

Up the steep hill, Jimmy and Gina walked pushing their way against a fierce blue wind. Jimmy's grandmother lived a few streets away. As they reached the top of the hill the sky rushed towards them and Gina looked out over the steep escarpment at the Edinburgh housetops.

Jimmy's grandmother possessed the same air of bleak realism as her grandson. A large picture of the crucifixion hung behind her chair. Two smaller pictures of a sad-eyed Virgin Mary stood on the dresser with rosaries hanging over them. One of Jimmy's uncles sat on the sofa. His greying hair touched his collar and he stared straight ahead as if he had recently suffered a shock. He was so full of methadone that he was incapable of speech. Everyone ignored him.

Jimmy went to make tea and Gina sat down next to his grandmother:

'Ye jist caught me. Ah'm on ma way tae ma neighbour's funeral. Gangrene,' she said approvingly. 'He smoked too much. Startit in his toes. Reached his bowel,' she added with grim satisfaction as she stubbed out her cigarette.

Jimmy brought in a tray of tea and some scones. His grandmother scanned Gina up and down. 'Jimmy tells me your frae Italy. We were in Rome once on a trip tae visit the Pope.'

Without warning, Jimmy's uncle got up and bolted from the room. The door of a back bedroom slammed shut.

Granny went on to recite a litany of disasters.

'It's ma neighbour's husband whose funeral Ah'm gawn tae. We went to see him on the Friday and he was breathin at a hundred and twenty-five miles an oor. We didnae see him when he brought a the blood up. We were in the cafeteria.' She looked critically at Jimmy. 'Jimmy Ah want ye tae go with me to the funeral. I jist want someone tae hawd ma arm gawn doon the steep bit of the hill.'

She looked at Gina's neat appearance with approval. 'Ye can come tae if ye wouldnae mind.'

Half an hour later the three of them walked down to the graveyard of the Sacred Heart church. Jimmy's gran wore her best blue hat. The burial service was already under way as they approached the graveside. Jimmy's gran crossed herself and gave a sympathetic nod to the assembled folk huddled together in the bitter cold. Just as the pall-bearers were lowering the coffin into the grave someone's mobile phone went off, playing a jazzy tune that cut through the silence. Jimmy's gran cast a look of outrage across the grave at the offender.

'Wull ye switch that thing awf. Huv ye nae respect?' she said sharply. 'There's a cunt lyin deid in that box.'

A dark navy-blue evening closed in over Edinburgh. Back in the flat Gina caught a glimpse through the half open door of Jimmy in the kitchen eating from a bowl. He ate with his eyes half shut in order to enjoy his food more. Her heart gave a lurch at the beauty of his pale ancient face as he spooned cereal into his mouth and there was some satisfaction in understanding that her mother had sacrificed herself to support people like him.

She returned to his mother's room and studied herself in the mirror. Then she checked once more on the yellow bag that lay beneath the bed and pushed it further out of sight. Last night she had dreamed of her mother. From the criminal glare in the police mugshots Gina had always assumed that her mother was a devotee of rage, living her life under a black cloud of fury. But in the dream her mother was laughing and looking down at a huge red flower that was opening out, unfolding its blood-red petals under her ribcage and radiating warmth. 'Look at this, Gina,' she was saying. 'Look at this.'

Jimmy hovered in the doorway. He came and sat next to her on the bed. His hand found its way to hers. His eyes were shining.

'Come intae ma room, eh?'

She allowed herself to be led into his room.

'I'd feel funny daein it in ma mam's room. Ah dinnae think she'd like it.'

Gina undressed with shivery excitement and slid into the cold bed. She pulled the duvet up to her chin. Jimmy went to wash his hands. He let himself back into the room, switched off the light and climbed into the bed with her.

In the early hours of the morning Gina lifted her head from the pillow, half awake. The room was filled with an unearthly pallor. A movement by the door caught her eye. Standing there was a figure that seemed to have squeezed itself out of the thin shadow of the door jamb. It was both solid and dissolving but with no distinguishable perspective or dimensions and it was shedding feathers of light. For a moment she thought it was Jimmy. Then she saw that from its head two wings folded themselves over its eyes. Two other wings spread from its shoulders and two smaller ones from its feet. The upper wings drew back for a moment to reveal two enormous eyes that consisted only of black pupils spreading right across the sides of its head.

Her mouth opened in astonishment. She reached out her hand to wake Jimmy. There was no-one in the bed next to her. It was empty. She sat up.

Jimmy was standing by the window.

'It's snowin,' he said.

'I've just seen something weird. Something with wings,' she gasped.

'It wis me,' he said and turned to her with a grin. 'I'm an angel. Aw, ma wing muscles are so sair.' He gave a mock shrug of his shoulders.

'No really. I saw something.'

'Yir just stoned,' he said matter-of-factly and pulled open the curtain.

Soft snow sifted steadily from the sky casting a pale light into the room.

The two brothers sprawled across the sofa watching *Scooby-Doo* on television. Gina poked her head round the door:

'I'm going to the Post Office to send a card.'

Jimmy smiled at her. Brian caught the smile and gave Jimmy a vicious jab in the chest with his elbow while using the remote control to flit from programme to programme.

In the street, flurries of fine snow stung Gina's cheeks. She posted a card to her workmates in Italy. When she came out of the Post Office she thought she saw the same creature unfolding itself from the corner of the betting shop next to the newsagent. But it was nothing more than tiny whirlwinds of snow. A bitter blast of freezing air rushed past her. At the same time a searing grief for her mother took her by surprise. She would deal with her mother's remains and then return to stay with Jimmy. Or perhaps he should come and stay with her in Italy. For the first time she thought she understood what her father had meant when he said her mother was on the side of the angels. Her boots crunched in the snow as she made her way back to the flat.

'Whit is it?'

When Gina returned Brian and Jimmy were standing in the front room looking at the jar containing her mother's brain, which was on the coffee table. The yellow bag had been thrown to one side. The brain bobbed about in the clouded water. Jimmy was whining in distress:

'Ye shouldnae hae gone into her room. Ah dinnae ken whit it is.'

Brian was looking at the jar with horror. 'Whit the fuck is it?'

Gina approached the table her face white. 'If you'll sit down for a minute I'll explain.'

They remained standing. The words rushed out:

'My mother . . . was in jail in Milan. They found her hanging in her cell. They took her brain out and sent it here to Edinburgh for experiments. I've come here to collect it.'

Brian collapsed back on the sofa screaming. He rolled over and put his hands up to cover his face:

'Just fuckin get it oot o here. Ah'm nae comin back till it's gone.' He jumped up and ran out of the flat slamming the door behind him. Jimmy stepped back unsteadily and tightened the belt around his jeans:

'Ye should hae told us, eh. Why did ye pit me in this situation?' he whimpered. 'I don't want somethin like that in the hoose. It maks me feel sick. People will think we're cannibals.'

Back in her bedroom she sat on the bed. Jagged triangular tears slashed at her cheeks.

A minute later she heard Brian coming back into the flat.

'It's fuckin' Baltic out there. Whaur's your jacket, Jimmy?'

'You're no havin it.'

There came the familiar sounds of a tussle and fierce yells. In the front room the boys faced each other. Brian's thin face was alight with sly hatred.

'Get rid of it. Our mam wouldnae like it. Ah'm your big brother. We've only got each other. She'd want me to look after ye. Mam wouldnae want it in the hoose. Get rid of it.'

'It's Gina's . . .'

'Fuck Gina. If you loved oor mam ye'll get rid of it. Gina's leavin anyway. I jus seen her packin.'

'Ye didnae.'

'Ah did. Go and look.'

Jimmy's skin prickled all over. He peeped through the open door of the bedroom. Gina was folding her clothes into a small case. He came back into the front room, his eyes large and dark. Brian stood watching. In one movement Jimmy grabbed the jar and pushed it into the yellow bag. Clutching the bag to his chest he ran out of the flat, leaping down the stairwell three steps at a time.

Suddenly he was flying through the hilly streets with tall tenement blocks towering like cliff glaciers on either side of him. Parked cars frozen into igloos. He was airborne, his ribcage a vessel full of air, the wind at his feet. At the top of the hill the rough ground fell away in a steep slope. Jimmy alighted. His eyes were black and enormous. His jaw cracked with the cold. With all his strength he hurled the bag and its contents over the railing and watched it falling away like a meteor until it lodged under some bushes, a fuzzy patch of yellow in the muddy undergrowth. In the distance the council garbage truck edged along the road. Council workers fanned out collecting litter and rubbish from the open snow-blanketed hillside.

Jimmy sat on a bench. After a while the cold got the better of him and he set off for home.

When he returned to the flat he found Brian and Gina in the front room. Her blonde hair was scraped back so tightly from her forehead it made her eyes bulge. Her bags were by her side.

'Ah telt her ye dumped it,' said Brian. 'She's booked her ticket back tae Italy.'

She turned a tearful gaze on Jimmy. 'Where is it?'

Brian smiled. Jimmy said nothing. The eyes of a panther looked out at her from his pale skin. She watched the bony-wings of his shoulder-blades shift as he pushed past her and went into his bedroom. The key turned in the lock.

'Will ah get ye a taxi tae the airport?' asked Brian politely.

SINGING IN THE DARK TIMES

It was a fine summer morning in June. Office workers streamed in and out of Finsbury Park tube station. Most people kept their heads down except for the tramp standing just outside the entrance. He was squinting up at the blue sky. He attracted attention because he was the only person who looked strikingly alive – albeit destitute. There was a burning vigour in his red cheeks that might have derived merely from exposure to open-air living, or from methylated spirits. Compared to the commuters, whose features seemed to have been modelled in soft wax, blurring any distinction between them, he stood out like a Rembrandt portrait – all warts and whelks, with a face that had been forged in adversity and realised by a master painter. He had a bushy head of grey hair, a broad nose threaded with a network of purple veins and he wore a greasy greatcoat – old army issue with umpteen pockets – that was tied around the waist with string. His eyes were bright blue but without lashes. Two strands of beads were visible under the collar of his coat.

Having finished examining the sky, he fumbled for an old leather shoe with the sole flapping off. This he held to his right ear and spoke into it as if it were a mobile phone.

'Hello. I'm in Finsbury Park. Where are you?' With his left hand he motioned passers-by impatiently towards the cap on the ground which had a few coins in it.

After a while, tired of this one-way conversation, he wandered over to a nearby parking meter to feel in the metal cavity for any forgotten coins. Returning to his post, he interrupted the flow of people to ask a man in black-rimmed spectacles for some change. The man swerved and hurried on.

'Piss off then you four-eyed twat,' the vagrant called after him cheerily.

From spring onwards, with the rising of the sap, all manner of tramps sprout up alongside the daffodils and by the summer they are bedding down in parks and doorways all over town. In the hierarchy of vagrants, Hoagy B, as he was known, considered himself to be somewhere near the top.

'I am a Tippel-Brother,' he would announce, should anyone ask. It was while stationed in Germany that he had come across the 'tippel-bruders'. They were known as 'orderly wanderers'. Their way of life appealed to him and he made a note of it for when he was de-mobbed. Apparently, in the glory days, there had been an International Brotherhood of Vagrants in Germany. To cap it all, Hamburg had even hosted a Vagrants Congress attended by three hundred of them. Rot set in when a vagrants' registration was introduced.

Hoagy B's main occupation was walking. For more years than he could remember, he had spent his time trudging from John O'Groats to Land's End and back again. He would go from farm to farm, getting fed for a days' work, cutting grass, house-painting, picking fruit, sometimes staying for up to a week and then heading off once more. When he needed money, he would venture into the nearest town and find casual work as a navvy, wielding a pickaxe or pneumatic drill on the roads for a while. But there was no work to be found in London this year and he had been reduced to a little light begging – not his preferred style.

He looked down at his watch and started back with a theatrical gesture as though the watch had affronted him in some way.

'Is that the time already?' he muttered.

This was all the more extraordinary because he had no watch. There was nothing on his wrist except a few pieces of string plaited together. Next to where he stood, his old brown nylon sleeping bag lay sodden after the night's rainstorm. As he held it up to inspect it the sleeping bag came apart in his hands. He kicked it into a doorway. Then he collected his cap, put the few coins in his pocket and set off.

A short while later he was seen striking out towards Hyde Park, now with an empty milk bottle to his ear, chatting in tandem with other members of the public who were also glued to their phones.

'Hang on. I can't roll a fag while I've got a telephone in my hand,' he said and stopped to throw the bottle in a litter bin before taking out his tobacco tin and continuing on his way.

Just before he entered the park something caught his eye. In a skip next to some iron railings was an old-fashioned Ferguson twelve-inch television. Hoagy fished it out and tucked it under his arm.

That June day the park was dotted with idlers in deckchairs, couples smooching on the grass and clerical workers tucking into their lunch-break sandwiches. Looking for a more secluded spot, Hoagy walked through Hyde Park and on to Kensington Gardens. There he took up residence on an empty park bench

sheltered by trees near the statue of Peter Pan. He put the television down on the ground and sat down. From one of his
pockets he pulled out a sock. In it were some hard-boiled eggs.
Then he rummaged until he found two other small packets
containing salt and pepper. After he had finished eating, he
cocked his legs up on the bench, put his arms behind his head
and gazed at the television.

A man shot by on a bicycle, his wispy white hair flying from
under an orange baseball cap. He sat upright and whistled as he
went. On his back he carried what looked like a canvas quiver
with multi-coloured plastic windmills poking out from the
top. When he spotted the tramp and the television, he put his
feet on the ground and skidded to a halt, then pushed himself
backwards towards Hoagy.

'Anything good on?' He was well-spoken with an amused
and slightly coquettish manner.

'Not much,' Hoagy replied. 'There's always something
missing when you're watching television, isn't there? It's the
woman coming round with ice creams.' The man rested his
bicycle against a tree and joined Hoagy who shifted along the
bench:

'I'm taking these windmills to the children of Grenfell.
They will want toys as well as blankets. Something beautiful,
eh? Bread and roses. We all have to do whatever we can. From
each according to his ability, to each according to his needs, as
they say. There's a collection centre in Walmer Road. Although
I hear they already have too much stuff.'

'What's happened at Grendel?' Hoagy enquired in a voice
that retained traces of a Welsh accent.

'No. Grenfell. Grendel's a different monster altogether.' The
man threw back his head and laughed. 'Beowulf defeated

Grendel. But the dragon hoarding the treasure was the one who did for Beowulf in the end. Kensington Borough Council in this case. Have you not heard about it? The tragedy? It was three days ago.'

'Can't say I have, Professor,' said Hoagy. He nodded towards the television. 'It weren't on the news.'

'Grenfell tower went up in flames.' All the laughter fell away from the man, who suddenly looked distraught. There was silence between the two for several minutes. A hard-boiled egg was pulled out from the sock and offered to the stranger who declined it with a shake of his head. Hoagy stood up and took a shining tin can from one of his pockets. He walked slowly over to the small lake opposite and helped himself to a drink of water.

Then, to the elderly cyclist's astonishment Hoagy turned to face him and began to sing, his chest expanding under the old army coat. Even more surprising, out of his mouth came a melodious and tuneful tenor voice:

'You've heard of the Gresford disaster
And the terrible price that was paid
Two hundred and forty-two colliers were lost
And three men of the rescue brigade.
Now the Lord Mayor of London's collecting
To help out the children and wives.
The owners have sent some white lilies, dear God
To pay for the poor colliers' lives.'

'Yes,' said the cyclist, the twinkle now back in his eye. 'You're right to sing. How does that quotation go? "In the dark times will there also be singing? Yes, there will also be singing –

about the dark times." Is that a trained tenor voice of yours I detect?'

'Yes. Once. A while back. Before the army,' Hoagy growled. He frowned and spat on the ground.

The cyclist put on his cap and bent to adjust his cycle clips. At that point a ladybird flew on to the frayed cuff of Hoagy's coat, folding its wings back under the scarlet and black dotted shell. He tried without success to shake it off. The man mounted his bicycle:

'I'll be on my way. Good luck.'

'And to you, sir.' Hoagy watched him cycle off. 'Fly away home,' he said to the ladybird, which did not move.

Several hours later Hoagy B found himself standing in Walmer Road. He looked up to see, a few blocks away, the towering blackened ruin. Shocked at the sight he backed into a doorway and rolled himself a cigarette. The street was noisy and crowded. People of all sizes and descriptions shouted encouragement to each other, pushing trolleys of bottled water and struggling with plastic bags full of clothes while others manhandled crates of soft drinks. Trestle-tables had been set up, piled with a variety of foods and fruits and yet more water bottles. Cars were parked skew-whiff in the road with their boots open as people ferried goods to various destinations.

The doors of the Westway Centre were wide open. Hoagy approached and peeped inside. Close to the doors were rows of charcoal grey sports mats and foam mattresses laid out in formal lines. Some contained sleeping figures. On others sat small family groups. There was a hum of organised activity. A short dark-haired woman stood on a chair directing proceedings, ordering a chain of helpers who were passing armfuls of bedding, blankets and sleeping-bags to each other. The woman shouted instructions:

'This bedding is surplus. Put it in a pile near the door. A van will collect the surplus and take it for storage in a warehouse. The table at the back is for toiletries, nappies etcetera.'

She gesticulated to show where everything should go while volunteers milled about helping wherever they could.

Two yards from Hoagy, a small boy of about nine with a saffron complexion and shining black eyes stood holding his grandfather's hand. The man wore a white calf-length tunic and red soft-soled slippers. He was in his fifties with a small white beard, a long nose and eyes as black though not as brilliant as his grandson's. He squatted down and spoke to a plump woman wearing a red salwar kameez who was seated on a mat behind him. The man said something to the boy in a language Hoagy did not understand. Then the boy spoke to one of the volunteers who was squeezing sleeping bags into their nylon holders and tossing them to one side:

'My mum says, where's the bathroom.'

The volunteer explained and the boy went and translated the answer to his mother who heaved herself up from the floor and made her way in the direction pointed out.

Hoagy edged towards the pile of sleeping bags: 'Are any of these going?'

The young woman flicked back her fair hair and looked at the tramp with suspicion.

'Are you a Grenfell victim?

'No.'

'Well, I'm really sorry but all this has been donated for Grenfell victims only. Sorry.' She went over to alert her colleagues to the unwanted arrival of a tramp. The little boy stared at Hoagy. The grandfather stroked his beard and asked his grandson what was going on. He bent his ear to listen then raised his eyebrows and lifted his palms upward in a gesture of helplessness.

A solid middle-aged black woman in a brightly patterned dress bore down on Hoagy. Full of righteous indignation she confronted him:

'Out. Out. Out. Please. We don't want freeloaders. People have lost everything here. We're all pulling together. The whole community is trying. You should be helping. Not scrounging. Go away please.'

Hoagy hesitated then pointed at the sleeping bags: 'I heard they were spare.'

At that point a balding council official who had been advised to remove his identity badge because of local hostility stepped smoothly forward.

'I'll deal with this.'

He gripped Hoagy by the arm and propelled him into the street.

'Isn't it funny,' Hoagy said as he was pushed out of the door, 'that all we derelicts have wonderful heads of hair and all you officials and bankers are bald. When did you last see a bald tramp?' Having nearly tripped as he was ejected, he stood outside on the road for a few moments to gather himself. It was early evening. The bustle in the street had subsided. Here and there people stood around in subdued groups, talking in lowered voices. A few blocks away the setting sun shone through the charred tower block, turning it a rusty reddish colour as if its DNA contained a memory of fire.

Hoagy started to walk away. He had gone fifty paces when there was a tug on his sleeve. He looked down. The boy with the lustrous black eyes was standing there, his arms barely able to hold the sleeping bag and the bedroll. Hoagy accepted them. The boy gave a skip and scampered off towards where the grandfather stood just outside the doors, watching out for the boy. Hoagy lifted his right arm to touch the side of his bushy hair in a sort of salute.

By the time Hoagy reached Latimer Road station it was dark. The train on the elevated track rattled and shook its way through the buildings. Each carriage was illuminated. Hoagy watched the train pass showing scenes of daily life: in one compartment a man read a newspaper; in another, a woman leaned across to wipe her child's face. Hoagy tipped his head sideways. That was how Grenfell Tower used to be, each compartment like one of the flats containing a scene of every-day life. The train was like a vertical section of Grenfell travelling on its side instead of going upwards.

He staked his pitch outside Latimer Road tube station. The station was closed. He sat on the pavement and unpacked the sleeping bag. It was brand new. He undid the leather straps of the bedroll and unfolded it to have a look before tying it up again. Then he leaned back against the wall of the station. The last train rumbled past. After a while he put the bedding down and stood up to shake his head and stretch his arms. He took some deep breaths and hummed a little as if trying to find the right key.

By nightfall most of the inhabitants of the Westway Centre had been found hotel accommodation. There were a few left to sleep as best they could on the mattresses provided. None of those who remained recognised what they were hearing but it penetrated the dreams of some and even those half-asleep were soothed by it. One woman sat up to listen, entranced. From somewhere not too far away came the sound, floating on the night air, of a beautiful tenor voice singing one part of the duet from Bizet's *The Pearl Fishers*. Long into the night the voice could be heard singing different arias and snatches of opera.

Having done the best he could, the next morning Hoagy made an early start and headed west towards Ealing and away from London.

www.sandstonepress.com

Subscribe to our weekly newsletter for events information, author news, paperback and e-book deals, and the occasional photo of authors' pets!
bit.ly/SandstonePress

facebook.com/SandstonePress/

@SandstonePress